Lucky

J.M. DABNEY

This book is a work of fiction. Names, characters, businesses, organizations, places, events and incidents either are the product of the author's imagination or are used fictitiously. Any resemblance to actual persons, living or dead, events, or locales is entirely coincidental.

Cover content is for illustrative purposes only. Any person depicted on the cover is a model.

ISBN-10:1-947184-05-9
ISBN-13:978-1-947184-05-3

DEDICATION

To the ones that loved my Hyper Hippie and his Ginger Bear.

AUTHOR'S NOTE

Although this is part of a series, Lucky is a complete stand
alone.
Trigger Warning: This title deals with past abuse, suicide,
and rape.

CONTENTS

1 ENTER THE HYPER HIPPIE

Lee "Lucky" Trenton adjusted his ear buds and lifted his sketchpad from atop a stack of tattoo mags. He winced as his slowly healing sprained wrist reminded him of his latest accident. Since he'd first started walking, he fell at least once a week. It didn't help that his long gangly frame and oversized feet made him a moving hazard. He looked like a fucking scarecrow and about as attractive as one too.

He had no misconceptions about the power of his looks. Odd in temperament, personality and shape, it was what it was. He'd hit his peak at sixteen reaching a super leanly muscled six-three and there his growing ceased. It wasn't so bad. At twenty-eight he worked with a world-renowned group of tattoo artists. He'd worked his ass off from apprentice to well-respected member of Twirled World Ink. So, he didn't have many complaints about where his life was going, well except one—Matt "Priest" Beall.

The sexy fucker was his co-worker of five years and had driven him to the point of sexual frustration induced insanity since Gib introduced the short, husky bear as the newest artist. When Priest entered the zone, no one rivaled his confidence and talent but introduce flirting, and the man went terminally shy. Priest also had the cutest fucking stutter he'd ever heard.

Not that Priest noticed him. Priest relegated him to best friend status along with the rest of the Twirled World Crazies. Priest was completely oblivious to his interest or clues. Lucky's frustration levels hit the point of pulling a fucking caveman, bashing Priest over the head and dragging him to his lair. Sadly, that probably wouldn't work either. Landon Phelps, the big boss' son, tried to offer him advice, but again the more he tried to make his intentions known the more clueless Priest became. So, in the end, he'd sworn Landon to secrecy and decided being around Priest was enough.

Although watching all those hot guys try to get at his man threatened to turn him homicidal. All types tried to make a play for Priest, big heavily tattooed Bears or pretty and perfect barely legal boys and every type in between. The only saving grace really was Priest didn't jump at the not so subtle invites. Although those blushes that stained Priest's tanned cheeks above his beard were like waving a red flag at a rampaging bull—it was all challenge. Lucky wasn't intimidating enough to scare them away or even make his claim on Priest appear serious.

Scary, the shop manager, with one terrifying glance got the men to start running, but Scary wasn't around all the time.

Scary owned a bar named Brawlers. The name was self-explanatory. The cops hated the place, but the bodies and blood were normally nowhere in sight, and no one would talk by the time they showed up.

He cursed as his mind wandered and brought his attention back to Priest who was handling the phones and desk, scheduling appointments and consultations. Aside from Trouble, who was exactly how he sounded, Priest was the best one to deal with the public. He tended to talk to himself and what came out wasn't always flattering, so Lucky was banned from all business except ink. Which suited him fine, he was ecstatic to spend his time drawing until they assigned him a client or one requested him.

His phone started repeating The Wicked Witch is Calling in a terrified shriek, and he grabbed his phone. He tugged his earbuds out as he stroked his thumb across the screen and answered. "Hello, Ma."

"How is my least fucked up child doing today?"

A picture of the five-foot-nothing hellion known as his mother flashed in his head. For all the innocuous appearance of Lily, she was the poster child for heavy medication. He loved the crazy bitch.

"Your least fucked up child hasn't broken a bone and the day is almost over." His friends snickered from across the room, and he flipped them off without even glancing at them.

He'd grown up in a household that subscribed to a rule of radical honesty. No lies and the only rule was don't have the cops come to the house. Which in hindsight he had to admit his parents were fucking geniuses—no rules equaled no rebellion.

"What about stitches?"

"I assure you I'm free of new scars." He probably jinxed himself.

"How's the sex life?"

From any other mother the question would sound weird and creepy, but in his house growing up conversations about sex were open and non-judgmental. He hadn't even come out. The day his family found out he was gay was when he brought his first boyfriend home when he was thirteen.

"I'm a fucking monk," he muttered with deep disgust.

"Pathetic, young one, truly pathetic. Even your personality-less brother is getting some."

"He only gets ass because he pays well for it." The old joke made his mother cackle. Linus was socially awkward but always had a new woman on his arm every time he came home.

"It's still getting laid."

"I know, I'm an utter disappointment."

"Yes, you are."

"Thanks, Ma, I love you too."

"I've allowed you to survive for twenty-eight years, I assure you that took a lot of moral fortitude."

His impending death was an old threat. Out of Linus and Lucky's twin sister, Leigh-Lou, he was the most like his parents.

"I am appreciative that you granted me my continued breathing. Now, what do you want?"

"We're having an intervention. Your father and I think it's time you lose that pesky virginity."

"Ma, I haven't been a virgin since I was fifteen. As well you know since you bought me the condoms because you said me breeding would lessen the IQ of the next generation of Trenton progeny. Although, being gay and breeding—"

"You haven't decided to spread the seed through IVF because I'm sorry to say my hopes are your sister will carry on the line."

The horror in her voice at the thought he'd want to bring a child into the world made him lose it. He ignored the eye rolls and strange looks he noticed when he spun his chair to catch sight of his best friends. They stared at him with something close to horror in their gazes. His family's antics were well known. Although he was careful to make sure none of his friends, especially Priest, were left alone with any of his family they were aware of the damaged genes he carried.

"Yes, Leigh-Lou would be best to have the next gen, I mean really her *men are good for only one thing philosophy* is bound to catch up with her." His highly sexual twin didn't believe in monogamy or relationships, as soon as a man mentioned the c-word she was gone before the third syllable was out of their mouths.

"Leave your twin alone, at least she isn't sniffing some dude's ass and doesn't have the balls to pounce on it."

"And people wonder why I'm weird."

"You're the normal one, that's why we stopped asking you to attend functions for my side of the family. We can only take so much embarrassment."

"Just call me the dark family secret. So, we've discussed the ban on me discussing future children with my non-existent partner. How much I'm an embarrassment. The disappointment in my sex life that is no better than a eunuch's, so what the hell did you want?"

"My mother-in-law is coming for her annual inspection, and as per her request, all the fruits of her son's loins must be in attendance so she may count piercings, tattoos and whether the fuck of the year matches the one from last year.

"I swear that woman lives to ruin my fun. Your father has already hidden my scarf skirts and tasseled pasties. The man has been living in sin with me for nearly thirty-five long years. It's like the fucker doesn't know me yet."

"Hid the tasseled pasties, he must die! What about the sequined middle finger ones I made you for Mother's Day when I was ten? I made them extra-large since you said we ruined your nipples. Those would fit the occasion." The gagging behind him made him snort. That's what they get for being nosy.

"Those too. Like I said, he's putting a crimp in my fucking style. He knew I was weird the night we met. He fooled me. If I knew about his boring family, I would've kept my panties on."

"Well, how could you resist his line about the dashboard lights bringing out the green in your eyes? Or how *Grateful Dead* just built the sexual tension to combustible levels?"

"So, you be there at one and don't be late. Wear a sleeveless shirt, holey jeans and make sure your dreads are extra high on your head. Do you have that six-gauge septum bone horn? Do you have a date? Maybe one you can bring on a leash? I can only take an hour of that woman before I gotta bring out the hookah."

"Should I pull a big brother and pick up a trick from the street corner?"

"Oh, you do love me," she squealed. "Make sure they look like a case of antibiotics waiting to happen. I'll make sure I get a case of antibacterial sanitizer and spray."

"Okay, I'll see you Sunday."

"I'm rather fond of you at the moment."

"I'm fond of you too, Ma." The call disconnected and the silence in the shop made him turn to catch the stares.

"What the fuck is wrong with your family," Scary demanded.

"Nothing, why?"

"I think I threw up in my mouth a bit," Trouble gagged and reached for the trash can.

"Dude, you've met my family. You love my mother."

"Not enough to know about her ruined nipples," Trouble screeched.

"A year of breastfeeding—" He ducked the arsenal of pens Trouble aimed at his head.

"Did your mother do high quantities of drugs when she was pregnant?" Zerk shook his head.

"I think she did a bunch of acid before the rabbit died."

"That would explain it."

"Fuck you, guys, my mother is a fucking saint."

"No, she's heavily medicated, but I think that started long before the kids." Zerk gathered up his stuff and backpack. "I'm going to the back. I'm destined to have nightmares tonight."

The big gruff man took off at a run. Scary wasn't far behind, but he wasn't running—just disgusted.

People would think something was wrong with his family. They were as normal as the next just with a few extra quirks.

"It wasn't that fucking bad," he yelled at Zerk's retreating form. "You ain't got something to say," he asked Priest.

"I like your mother."

"That's because I've never left you alone with her. You're coming to dinner this Sunday."

"Oh—no, no I can't do that. Your sister grabbed my—" Priest lowered his voice. "—junk last time. She's been texting me for months. I still don't know how she got my number."

"She swiped it from my phone. Doesn't matter you're coming. I'll give you mace. It won't put the she-devil down for long, but it'll give you enough time to make a run for it and scream for help."

"Maybe a taser or better yet a cattle prod, that way he won't have to get close to her. She gets within a few feet, he can shock her." Trouble set the trashcan back down and sent Priest a sympathetic look.

"That's my sister, man."

"Yeah, I know, but it's true. I screamed at her I was gay the first time I met her because the sex-starved expression made me feel dirty. I thought I was gonna need a shower."

"Yeah, the shrieked panic coming out when five-foot of nothing wasn't even near you wasn't unmanly at all. If I remember, you shoved your innocent boyfriend in front of you like a shield."

"Brody is bi, he's seen pussy before."

"Her pussy wasn't out. Her skirt wasn't that short."

"Dude, we could almost see if she waxed—" Trouble gagged.

"I'm going to get coffee."

"Pick me up—"

"No, you're on your own. Get your pretty husband to get you your coffee. Priest, you want something," he asked the silent man.

"Thanks, my usual. Do I really have to go with you Sunday?"

"Yes," Lucky answered and left the shop. Then what he'd done hit him. Priest attended plenty of Lucky's family dinners, but not when the Grand Monster made her yearly inspection. He was going to subject Priest to full-on family crazy dysfunction. The only thing he could hope was his family kept his secret, but secrets and lies never remained hidden. He was fucked and not in the way he wanted to be, fucking great. Bribes, he needed lots and lots of bribes or spiked drinks. If they were sleeping, they couldn't talk. The thought buoyed his spirits, and he smiled to himself with a plan forming.

2 PRIEST'S CRAZY BEST FRIEND

Priest glared at the dark circles under his eyes and tried to ignore the emptiness he saw staring back at him. The night terrors were quickly tearing him apart. He clicked off the light over the bathroom sink and walked out of the bathroom. It was almost four a.m., and he'd slept only a few hours before he'd felt hands around his wrists and lips pushing so hard against his he tasted blood as teeth cut into the lower curve. He'd fought hard, tried to scream, but it was always silent. Like four years ago, there wasn't anyone there to save him, he'd been alone in his fear for three years before that. He relived each painful push of hips, one set after another until he'd shut his mind down.

He absently rubbed the long scars hidden under the ink on his forearms. Priest hadn't cut deep enough that night, and his mother found him only to scream her disappointment. She believed what happened to him was punishment for his deviant lifestyle. Afterward, even when she drove him to the emergency room, he knew part of her wanted to leave him there alone in that bathtub.

The first door he came to he stopped and pushed it open, Lucky always slept with it cracked open. Priest knew he did it on purpose for nights like that. He stepped into the room that was illuminated by a purple lava lamp and padded softly to the bed. Lifting the covers, he slipped in beside Lucky and quickly but as gently as possible he lined his body up beside Lucky. His friend's arm instantly wrapped around him and rolled Priest closer.

"Shh, just go back to sleep," Lucky whispered the words against his forehead as a soft kiss brushed his skin.

He let out a shuddered breath and hugged Lucky's middle.

"Come on, baby, relax."

"I'm sorry, I shouldn't—"

"Stop, I leave the door open for you. I'd wish like fuck you'd talk to me, but I won't force you. It's your business if you want to share."

"Not tonight."

"No problem, man, tomorrow night or a year from now. My bed is yours whenever you need it."

"Thanks."

Long, slender fingers with slight callouses soothingly stroked along his ribs. Years went by without him letting anyone touch him even in a casual way until Twirled and Lucky. For all the mean, rough biker appearances they were an affectionate crew. He'd almost had a panic attack the first time Zerk threw his arm over his shoulder and Priest thought he'd held it together well, but Zerk had slowly pulled away.

There was something about Lucky though. There was always safety in his presence. Lucky even went out of his way to touch him all the time, but the other man never made him feel frightened or hunted. All the other men that took his natural shyness as a challenge. It barely had him holding onto whatever strength he'd gathered in the last few years.

"Go to sleep, I can fucking hear you thinking."

"Sorry."

"Don't be sorry, ain't nothing to be sorry about, but I've heard you walking the house the last few nights. Plus, you gotta have all the rest you can get, you get to spend the afternoon with my family."

"Do I—"

"Yes, you have to, I ain't going there by myself. Plus Ma told me to bring a tattooed, totally inappropriate date to make the mother-in-law run. Grams loses her shit when Ma brings out the bong just to deal."

He snickered. "It can't be that bad."

"Oh fuck, you got no idea. The woman lives to make Ma's life hell. Ma didn't grow up in a different class bracket, she grew up on an entirely different planet."

"Your Mom's not that bad. I've always found her to be sweet even in her weirdness."

"Thanks, man. She ain't for everyone. She likes you though."

He hid his smile, but a memory pushed it away. "My mother never liked me."

"That's bullshit. No one cannot like you, it's fucking impossible."

"I don't remember a time when she hugged me or smiled at me. She told me I was a deviant pervert."

"Ain't anything deviant about you. So you like dick? I do too."

"You never bring anyone home." He didn't want to admit he was secretly thrilled Lucky never brought any of his tricks home. Okay, he wasn't stupid enough to think Lucky went without. Lucky was sexy as hell, maybe not in a traditional sense, but nonetheless sexy.

Anyone looking at him would think Lucky was skinny, but under all his baggy handmade hemp clothes was a leanly muscled body. Even now perfect six-pack abs moved under his arm. Lucky was heavily pierced and tattooed just like the rest of the crew, and he had his ears stretched to a 00 gauge. Like his hemp clothes, he wore natural jewelry in wood, stone or bone. Lately Lucky was favoring glass ones with tinted skull inlays.

"No reason to bring them home when I know I ain't going to keep them around."

"Why not?" He regretted the question as soon as it was out of his mouth.

Lucky stiffened against him, "I kinda met someone, but it ain't going anywhere."

"Oh, you've never told me."

"It's no big deal. Sometimes we just don't fucking get what we want."

"Yeah." He fell into silence and closed his eyes.

Priest focused on the steady beat of Lucky's heart as it lulled him into sleep. Maybe a few hours of uninterrupted sleep would make him feel human. He tried not to dwell on the fact the only place he could sleep without the dreams was in Lucky's arms. One day when Lucky's secret man stopped being stupid, Priest wouldn't even have these brief moments of comfort and peace.

♦♦♦

Chimes tinkled in every direction as he looked around the yard of Lucky's parent's home. Two kegs with the tops cut off and holes cut in random patterns set on either side of the porch steps with colorful flowers cascading down the sides. Recycled tires were used as planters all over the yard, there was an old, claw-foot tub turned into a fountain, bird bath combo and an old rusted out Model-T covered in climbing roses and ivy vines. Even at first glance, the yard and house you knew a unique family lived there. Priest loved coming there to spend time with the Trentons.

Lucky held tight to his hand as the man dragged him up the old, tile mosaic walkway and up the steps to the porch. "Don't make eye contact and whatever you do, don't run they'll consider it a challenge."

"I've been here before. They're not that bad, Lucky."

"Oh fuck, yes, they are."

Lucky didn't wait for him to answer and pushed open the door, the familiar scents of incense and weed perfumed the interior. Ma Lily started early. He chuckled but bit his lip when Lucky gave him a dirty look. Okay, he understood Lucky didn't come from a normal family and the whole radical honesty was kind of weird, but there was one thing that couldn't be denied—it was a loving family.

"Look at my boy, have you trimmed your dreads?"

"No, Ma, they are actually an inch longer than last time you asked."

"Doesn't look like it. Have you changed your cologne? It smells—unnatural."

"No, Ma, no deodorant or cologne—all natural."

"You know they kill animals to make all those products."

"Yes, yes, bunnies lose eyeballs for people's cruel need to smell good for sex when sex smells are the best smells. All sweaty and musky."

"I raised you right. Priest, how's my pretty, little bear?" Lily bypassed Lucky to wrap her arms around him. Even had five-nine the woman barely came to his chin.

"Hi, Lily, thanks for having me today."

"Oh, honey if I had you, you'd know it."

He couldn't answer because his throat tightened and he sent Lucky a panicked look. The bastard only snorted.

"Ma, didn't your open relationship days end a long time ago?"

"Yes, that worked better for my parents than me. Who knew the sperm donor wouldn't be able to share?"

"He's an only child. It's to be expected. Now unhand my man, you're making him nervous."

"Oh, why do I make him nervous? Really, so that nice bulge is only for you?"

"You know he's only my friend and his bulge ain't any of your business."

"Shame because he does have a nice one."

He found himself pried from Lily's tight embrace and placed behind Lucky. The open conversations about sex always made him uncomfortable, but it was kind of nice to see a family so open and positive about it. He gripped the side of Lucky's shirt. As always it was ultra-soft, all-natural fabrics and sleeveless. His jeans hung low on his hips precariously held up by intricately knotted strings of hemp with a dreaded skull buckle.

"Get Priest's bulge out of your brain."

"Woman, are you molesting Priest again? When did you develop a clergy fetish?"

"If they looked like Priest I'd give up my heathen atheist ways."

"Dad, didn't you remember she needed a ball gag for polite company?"

"Son, the ball gag is for the bedroom only."

"Please, I came over unexpectedly a few weeks ago to find you and your Shabari session going on."

"Sexual spice keeps a relationship healthy."

"As you've always told us. So, where's Linus and his clinic visit waiting to happen?"

"He's in the kitchen, and I swear I don't know where he finds them."

"I heard he likes to troll Oliver Ave."

"I swear this one's wearing dominatrix gear under her excessively tight dress."

He snickered from behind Lucky, and he nearly squeaked when the distinguished gentleman peeked around Lucky to see him.

"Hello, Priest, he's not exactly big enough to use as a shield."

"Hi, Damon."

"Come on, son, let's go make jokes that will go over Linus' date's head. She has this nasally giggle. I think it's caused by too much coke, but she's really testing the radical honesty rule in this house." Damon held out his elbow, and he slipped his arm through it.

"Don't try to steal him from me."

"Just because I'm bi doesn't mean I want your pretty man."

"Uh huh, you getting all fucking gentlemanly and giving him that flirty smile. I know you, old man, I will end you."

"So possessive, how do you put up with him, honey?"

"He doesn't give me a choice."

"Traitor," Lucky bellowed behind him as Damon led him toward the kitchen and into the backyard.

"Oh, I think she's fucking worse than the last one." The purple wrap dress looked to be about a size too small, and the six-inch spiked heels were sinking into the grass threatening to tip the woman backward.

"I thought so too. For such an intelligent man, Linus isn't very bright."

"Maybe he's just lonely."

"Lonely can be cured. Linus, Lucky brought his man."

"Priest, you still putting up with my brother? I've always wanted to know are you high?"

Linus wasn't always the nicest man to be around especially when it came to Lucky. He didn't understand it. Maybe the man just didn't think he fit with the rest of them. The suit Linus was wearing cost more than Priest paid in rent for a year. "No, Lucky is perfect."

"Definitely high."

"Where'd you pick this one up?"

"Don't even start with your fucking hooker jokes. I work with her."

"I don't think I mentioned hooker, that was all you."

"Dominique, this is Priest my brother Lucky's boyfriend."

He didn't even bother to correct Linus. Everyone called him Lucky's boyfriend since his first visit. He'd corrected them so many times that first visit and the next, then gave up because they didn't stop.

"It's nice to meet you." The woman practically sneered at him and ignored his extended hand.

"Yeah, the snarled nose like you're smelling shit on your shoes screams nice to meet me." He'd pushed the words through clenched teeth, and he turned to find Damon affectionately smiling at him, and the older man squeezed Priest's hand that was still tucked into the crook of his arm.

"Linus, everything go well at your last clinic visit? The itching and burning stopped? Antibiotics are a modern marvel."

Dominique perked up when she looked over his shoulder, and he knew what she saw, Lucky approaching with his naturally lazy swagger.

"Why are you all over my man, Dad, come on." Lucky wrapped his arms around his waist and lifted him a few feet away from Damon.

"Shut up, Lee," Linus snarled. "Leave the jokes alone today."

"Yeah, united front for the evil Gram monster, did you bring it?"

"You know I fucking did, here, I can never get the damn things right." Linus dropped something in Lucky's extended, open palm. "I'm so out of fucking practice with this shit."

"Won't exactly go with the spiffy suit. Didn't you bring a chance of clothes?"

"Yes, I had a work meeting before I got here. Just put the fucking things in."

"Give me that, you got the pliers?" Priest took the baggie with the eyebrow ring and the thick steel ring for Linus' nose.

"When don't I have pliers, the ER would ruin my fucking shit if I let them take them out."

The small thin nosed pliers came to rest on his palm. "Do I need gloves?"

"Don't you start too, you're the only normal one I have to deal with here."

He rolled his eyes. With quick, efficient movements he reinserted the eyebrow ring and tightened the ends around the ball, making sure the points lined up with the indentations. The next was the septum ring. "We should get you a septum horn, that would be so much easier just a simple insert."

"I know, but I never wear the stuff anymore."

"I'll order you one, I'll let Lucky know when it's in, and you can come and pick it up."

"Thanks, we only do this shit when Gram comes to visit."

"It makes Lily happy." He finished up and realized Lucky had never moved away from him, his slender body was still pressed against his back.

"Priest, come help me in the house," Lily called from the back deck.

"Okay, behave while I'm gone."

"Yeah, yeah, don't start ruining my fun."

He chuckled as he jogged to the porch. "What can I help you with?"

"I need a couple of boxes moved."

"Okay." He followed her toward the back of the house. He walked into what he knew was her bedroom.

"Priest, we have to talk."

"What," he asked as he heard the legs of a dresser scrape loudly across the floor and he turned to find himself trapped. "What—what are you doing, Lily?"

"This is really for yours and Lucky's own good."

"What's for our own good?"

"An intervention. It's been a long time coming."

Priest looked around for an escape, but he didn't see a way out except the windows. He knew she'd try to stop him and he'd never do anything to hurt Lily. A loud thump and a curse, then thundering steps alerted him that Lucky was coming to his rescue.

3 IT'LL ATTACK IF YOU MAKE EYE CONTACT

"Son, don't get mad, this is for your own good."

Lucky shot his dad a shocked look and then glanced toward the house as he watched his mother lock the door and smile at him.

"What the hell is the crazy harpy doing?"

"Didn't we say intervention?"

"Dad, Priest doesn't know how to protect himself, you've sent an innocent into the den of crazy." He took off running even as he yelled over his shoulder. She may have locked the fucking door, but the windows were never locked. He forced one of the windows open and dive-jumped through it, his shoulder crashed into a heavy shelf, and he grunted in pain.

Jogging down the hallway to his parent's room he tried the door, it wasn't locked, but wouldn't open. "Ma, did you put furniture in front of the door?"

"We know you pick locks. This has to be done."

"Lucky, what the hell is going on?"

"Baby, curl into a ball and play dead until she's bored. It'll be over soon."

He peeked through the tiny crack in the door and then pressed his ear to it to see if he could hear what was going on. Dammit, he should have known she'd try something. Three years of putting her off, of pretending that he was happy with friends, and all the times he made sure they were never alone. It all fucking ended now. She was going to ruin the best friendship he'd ever had.

"Priest, I just wanted to talk to you without my son running interference."

"Interference?"

"Don't engage the wild beast."

"Shut up, Lucky, this is between me and my boy."

"He's not your boy, he's mine, now back away from him slowly and let me in."

"No, I've done this your way, it's over with."

"Why are you peeking into Ma's room," Leigh-Lou asked from beside him, and he looked to find her leaning back against the wall beside the door.

"She's got Priest trapped in there."

"You knew she'd do this sooner or later. You're the only one that's going to give her a son-in-law."

"She doesn't fucking get it. She doesn't know."

"There's something you didn't tell Ma? Are you fucking insane? You know what happens when she finds out about lies by omission. She goes insane. She's like a fucking shark in a feeding frenzy."

"You're not fucking helping, now shut up so I can hear."

"You've been coming around for two years and you know I love you like you're one of my own, but what you and Lucky have isn't healthy."

"Ma, shut the fuck up, this isn't your business."

"I will poke your eye out or pierce your eardrum if you don't keep quiet."

"Threats of violence are beneath you." If he could just keep her distracted, she'd grow bored. The fucking woman had the attention span of a gnat on speed, but she'd also been stewing about this one for too long.

"I know what you're doing."

"Of course you do, this is why radical honesty sucks as a parenting model. Ma, I'm begging you don't do this, you don't know what's going on."

He hollered as an air horn went off on the other side of the door.

"Why the fuck do you have that?"

"It comes in handy sometimes. Now I'm talking to Priest and ignoring you." Lucky turned and slid down the door to sit on the floor. Leigh-Lou quickly joined him.

"Why didn't you ever tell her?"

"Because Priest hasn't even told me yet, I just put things together."

"Quiet, we won't be able to hear them."

He nodded at Leigh-Lou, and they pressed their ears to the crack. He'd always assumed what made Priest so jumpy or attributed to his night terrors. Saying the words, voicing his thoughts just talking to Leigh-Lou had caused his chest to hurt.

"She barricaded the door?" Linus slid down the wall on his opposite side and leaned his head back.

"Yep."

"Shh, she's talking," Leigh-Lou hushed them, and they all three focused on what was happening in the room.

"Do you know why I practice radical honesty with my kids?"

"No, I assumed that's how you grew up."

"No, when I was growing up I lived in a house of lies. My parents hid who they were, they were very much like Damon and myself, unconditional love, but for many years I thought they simply cheated on each other. Until I confronted them when I was seventeen about their affairs, and they told me they preferred an open relationship. But years of living with half-truths—"

"Disillusioned you?"

"Definitely. You live a daily lie, and Lucky's told me you spend more nights in his bed than in your own. Comfort is all well and good, but soon that comfort becomes a—"

"Ma, back the fuck off—"

"Don't make me air horn your ass again," she hollered from the other side of the door.

Lucky sighed when his twin leaned toward him to rest her head on his shoulder, and he leaned his cheek against her soft hair. She gripped his hand and, just like a majority of their life, they didn't need to open their mouths to communicate. Even Linus scooted over until his brother's hip was pressed against his and they were kids again, the three weird kids against the world. The ones with the hippie clothes and protest tees, the ones who spent weekends and summers at communes and music fests.

"Please don't do this, Ma." Lucky wasn't above begging to save Priest from remembering pain and fear that still haunted him years later. He'd fallen in love with the man much too quickly and each night Priest slept soundly curled up to him it was a sweet agony that existed between contentment and torture.

"Speaking about the pain makes sure it doesn't fester. You're a handsome and sweet man, my son adores you and couldn't live without you."

"He'd do fine without me. He's perfect."

"Son, I swear you're higher than I fucking am."

"Lily, I get you want to help, but there's nothing that can be done for me. I'm a lost cause, and Lucky's my best friend."

"Don't you want more than friends?"

Lucky held his breath and waited for Priest's answer. He's waited two years to find out if the man felt even half of what Lucky felt for Priest. Fuck, he seemed to get more pathetic every day.

"He's my friend, nothing more."

Those five words broke Lucky's heart, assuming something isn't like knowing it, and now he knew.

"Can I have my man back now?"

"I'm getting tired of you, Lucky."

"Now you know how I feel."

"Why do you think you can only have friends and I'm not talking just about Lucky."

What he heard next he struggled to make out the words because Priest was practically whispering. "I'm used and broken."

"Bullshit. Just because some man—"

"Men, there were several of them."

"Everyone has bad relationships. That's what makes the right one so much better."

"It wasn't really a relationship, okay," Priest voice rose and broke a bit. "Five men held me down and took everything from me. Took my first. Took my confidence.

Took what I was and ruined me, I put a razor to my wrists, and I even fucked that up. My own mother was disappointed I failed."

"Oh, Priest," Lily's voice broke and faded.

"What, not what you thought? Just thought some man did me wrong, maybe knocked me around. Did it make your radical honesty complete?"

"Priest, baby." Lucky stood up, and with the help of his brother and sister, they pushed the door until the legs of the dresser scraped across the floor. He ran into the room and took Priest into his arms. He spared his mother a glance and saw the tears in her eyes.

"Look at me, baby." He placed his hands on Priest's cheeks and lifted his teary eyes to his. "You're not used or ruined, you're fucking perfect. From the top of your shaggy head to the tips of your ugly toes. Nothing about you is broken." He kissed Priest's forehead, his eyes and tasted the salty tears, and then each cheek. "You are perfect, handsome, and talented. If you'd succeeded in taking your life, even if I had never met you some part of me would have always wondered why a piece of me was missing. You were meant to be my best friend, meant to be here. I love you, Priest." He pressed the lightest kiss on Priest's plump lips.

"I'm not per—"

"Yes, you are. I'm like the hippie George Washington, I can't tell a lie. You didn't offer those fuckers your first time, as far as I'm concerned, your first time is up for offer. And the man that gets you will be fucking lucky to have you. You fucking understand me?" The crying man nodded his head the best he could because Lucky held tighter to his cheeks, stroking the surprising softness of his beard.

28

"Give me my boy." Lily pushed between them and wrapped her arms tight around Priest's shoulders. "That woman isn't your mother, no more, you were mine the moment you walked through that door with Lucky. We ain't much, but we love you, even that douche bag Linus. He's adopted anyway."

Lucky felt a bit lighter when he heard a soft laugh coming from Priest. What happened to Priest was worse than what his imagination conjured. He thought a past abusive boyfriend had made his man skittish. The thought that men held Priest down and took, he shook his head. No one else was having Priest. The man had been created for him alone. He wasn't any kind of prize, but he loved Priest and not as a friend. Soon enough Priest would learn that, but for now, his baby needed some TLC and Lucky would give him everything he needed.

"Now, let's go out back, have a few hits before the Evil One arrives, it'll be soon, I felt a shift in my Chakras. She approaches, I bet she's leaving a trail of charred footsteps and dead animals in her wake. Until then, we can make fun of that harpy Linus brought home. If he'd just admit he was gay and find a nice boyfriend, we wouldn't have to deal with this shit. I mean, really, Lucky's so gay his aura is a rainbow and Leigh-Lou's slip-in-slide has had so many riders I'm sure it's so dry it would take skin off now, and we still love them."

"We love you too, Ma," Leigh-Lou and Linus muttered and exited the room

"Now, that the adopted ones left..." Lily sat sideways on Priest's lap. "So, do you want to be a Trenton?"

"The normal one doesn't seem to survive with y'all."

"Bullshit, I've let Lucky live. Besides you'd be my favorite."

"Okay."

"Yes, I'll go let Damon know he can't lust after you anymore. You being our son that would just be creepy unless you have a Daddy thing."

"No," Priest squeaked.

"Good, now, don't have sex in my bed." Lily smacked a kiss on Priest's cheek and left.

"I'm sorry. If I'd fucking known she'd pull this shit I'd never brought you here."

"I know you wouldn't. You won't tell—"

"What happened here is between us, it isn't their business. Want to catch one before the Gram monster shows up?"

"No, but I could really use a beer."

"You got it, come on, baby." Lucky slipped his arm around Priest's waist, stood and brought Priest with him.

Soon Priest would be his in every way. The man just didn't know it yet.

4 PRIEST'S CUDDLE THERAPY

He settled deeper into the thick cushions of the lounger chair and propped his bare feet on the deck railing. The book he'd attempted to read for the last hour laid open on his thigh. Priest couldn't put out of his mind what happened at the Trentons' days before. He hadn't spoken of what his ex had done to him outside his therapist's office since the night he'd tried to kill himself.

Three years he'd lived with his ex-boyfriend, and every day seemed like hell until that last night when he'd learned how much of a psycho the man was when he'd refused to be a toy for his friends again. The first time had been bad enough, and he barely survived it—the second time would've broken what was left of him. His ex and friends had taken his first time in the most brutal way possible. To want to repeat it proved he'd lived with a monster, but no matter how sick it made Priest seem, he'd been young and just wanted to be loved.

The nightmares were worse, and he'd resisted sleeping in Lucky's bed. Like the pathetic man he was, he'd paced outside the door. He laid his head back and closed his eyes.

Out of everything Lucky said to him when him and his siblings pushed into Lily's room, the one thing he couldn't forget or process was Lucky said he loved him. He knew it was in a friend's only capacity, but he wanted so much more.

"Don't you have a therapy appointment today?" Lucky's voice had sounded seconds before a hand gripped his ankle and Lucky was between his legs with his back to his chest.

"Yeah, in a few hours."

"No time for a nap then, I'm going with." Lucky absently wrapped Priest's arms around him.

Gentle fingertips turned one of his wrists up to trace scars covered with black ink. Equally tender lips brushed against them—the hesitation marks and then the final long cut.

"Wha-what do you mean you're going with me?" He rested his chin on the surprisingly soft texture of Lucky's dreadlocks. He inhaled deeply of comfortingly familiar scents of Lemon shampoo and Lucky's favorite incense.

"We're going to a Cuddle Therapy thing Ma suggested, gotta ask that head shrinker of yours if that's okay."

"Cuddle Therapy?" His voice squeaked in a totally unmanly fashion.

"It's a workshop thing. Touch. Cuddling. Exploring intimacy and communication. There's a bunch of activities or some shit. Ma said it worked for a friend she met at yoga."

"I can't cuddle with strange people."

"People pay money to cuddle and get cuddled. I could get a second job, man, I'd cuddle the fuck outta someone."

Priest felt his lips twitch. "I already like cuddling with you."

"Not the last few nights. Hurt my fucking feelings actually. Because Lily fucked up doesn't mean I gotta get punished for it."

Lucky sounded hurt. He'd always thought his friend humored him about Priest slipping into his room at night. Lucky was his best friend, of course, he was going to help, but did the man need it as much as him?

"It's no one's fault. Lily didn't know what happened and neither did you. I've been a bit raw lately."

"I get that, man, I do, but pushing me and the guys away is a dumb ass move."

"That wasn't my intention. There was just some shit I had to get straight in my head first."

"No excuse."

"Um, I don't know if it's a good idea if you're in the same room as a psychiatrist and a script pad."

"Naw, man, it was only a seventy-two-hour hold last time. As soon as they got a look at my family, I was out. It was kinda cool actually. I met this dude inside. Awesome as fuck stories."

Priest couldn't help it, he started laughing and tightened his arms around Lucky. "Only you'd see the bright side of a psych hold."

"There's worst shit in the world."

"Agreed, but you really want to go to my appointment?"

"Yeah, why?"

"I talk about...stuff."

"Of course you do, it's a shrink."

"Are you going to behave?"

"I can't make a promise unless I know I can follow through. Gotta keep the Karma clean."

"Your Karma?"

"Yeah, I won't even kill a bug. I don't wanna go totally Kafka in my next life."

"So, you think you'll come back as a huge bug?"

"You know aliens are out there, they could come down to Earth and bump some alien uglies with some human chicks, hell, they're E.T.s so might even go after the dudes. I ain't gonna be someone alien's host's spawn."

"You think about this a lot."

"Nope, just thoughts that pop into my head."

"About insect aliens coming down to Earth to mate with human males and females to breed an insect race?"

Lucky shrugged and settled deeper in the V of his legs. "You're weird."

"It's one of my best qualities."

"Maybe."

He sighed heavily and again leaned his head back. Closing his eyes right then wouldn't be a good idea. Priest would fall asleep in seconds. He didn't understand how quick Lucky could put him at ease. The majority of people who met Lucky believed him to be crazy. To be honest, it was one of the reasons he didn't want Lucky to go with him, but it wasn't the main reason. His best friend didn't know all the details of what happened, and he didn't want him to hear.

The first time he'd met Lucky, Gib introduced them and Priest extended his hand to shake, instead, Lucky pulled him in for a back breaking hug. He'd waited for the panic and for his lungs to seize up, yet that never happened. All he'd felt was an instant calm and rightness, neither of which he'd ever experienced before. And it had only intensified each day that past.

"Quit trying to think of ways to get out of taking me. It ain't fucking happening."

"I didn't think it would. Let me up so I can go take a shower and get ready." He pushed at Lucky's slender yet broad shoulders until he started to grumble.

"Fine, but I was comfortable." Lucky rolled to his feet.

"We can curl up and take a nap when we get home."

"You're just trying to get me into bed."

"Would I do that," Priest asked.

"No, but a man can fucking hope. Get up. We got shit to do."

Before he could respond, Lucky already disappeared into the house. What did he mean by a man could hope? No, Lucky didn't lie or filter what he said. If his friend wanted him, he'd blurt it out at the most inopportune moment, wouldn't he? Yes, Lucky treated him differently—affectionately. He shook his head and swung his legs off the lounger to stand. He'd dissect his fucked up thoughts later.

♦♦♦

Priest's knee bounced as he stared at Dr. Campbell as she warily watched Lucky. "Matt, you've never invited a guest into one of our sessions before. Would you like to tell me why today?"

"Lucky has a question for you, and he insisted."

"Okay, what's the question?"

"Oh, yeah, my Ma was at Yoga, and she was flirting with the chick she knows. They ain't fucked as far as I know, and she tells us everything."

For a psychiatrist, the doctor's eyes were getting wider by the second.

"And that has something—"

"Well, the chick has intimacy issues, no problem with fucking because for some that's just a physical, biological act. An exchanging of fluid and all that shit."

"Lucky," Priest said his name and placed his hand on his thigh.

"Okay, well, she, the chick, not my Ma, went to one of those workshops. Where people cuddle and touch to explore intimacy, no sex. Well, I guess they could fuck if they were so inclined, they're adults and all that."

Priest cleared his throat.

"I wanted to know if it would fuck up Priest's—"

"Priest," Dr. Campbell asked.

"Oh, yeah, Gib gives us all names when we start. Matt was all proper and shit, rarely heard the man cuss. Kind of unnatural if you ask me—off track. I wanted to take Matt and wanted to make sure it would be okay."

"I don't see why it would be a problem. It's in some ways a trust exercise. Which I know Matt has an issue with, but what do you think him cuddling with other—"

"Oh fuck no, only me, not that I wouldn't like to get a job as a professional cuddler because I told Priest I'd cuddle the fuck—"

"Off track again."

"You fucking ruin all my fun, Priest."

"No, I don't."

"You wouldn't let me make hooker jokes about the prostitute Linus brought to Sunday dinner."

"She wasn't a prostitute, I do think she actually works with your brother."

"Well, what about that dude Leigh-Lou brought?"

"I didn't stop you from telling him that Leigh-Lou was going to dump him five minutes after dinner."

"You know she can't commit, I was trying to save him from getting too attached, and he was acting some lovesick puppy. You could see the disgust in her eyes. Besides he wasn't good stud stock."

"She's not breeding. She made it perfectly clear."

"She's young."

"She's your twin."

"Semantics, she's ten minutes younger than me."

"Excuse me." Dr. Campbell waved her hands to get their attention. "Can I ask you some questions, Lucky?"

"Sure, I don't lie so be careful what you ask."

"Everyone lies."

"Nope, raised with radical honesty, good or bad, truth is the only thing my family speaks."

"People lie, sometimes for good reasons, but more often it's bad."

"Why lie? I mean what's the point in it. The truth hurts sometimes, but if in the end, it has good intentions then isn't it worth it?"

"So, you've never lied to your parents, even about something as small as why you missed curfew?"

"Never had a curfew."

"What about when you wanted to go somewhere, but your parents said no, and you did it anyway."

"Um, nope, we came and went as we pleased."

"Your first sexual experience?"

Oh God, he braced himself because he knew that was going to spiral out of control. Lucky's favorite subject was sex.

"Came home and told the parents, Ma bought me the condoms said I was unfit to breed, but being gay I told her it was kinda pointless, I just didn't want the clap. The guy was older and more experienced. You never know where someone's been."

Priest swore Dr. Campbell started to choke but covered with a cough and a sip from her coffee cup.

"Sex is natural. Fetish is Fetish some weirder than others, but whatever helps you get it up or stroke one out. Mom and Dad tried an open relationship for awhile. Quite a few boyfriends and girlfriends for both, Dad's bi and Ma isn't choosy. Getting off is getting off.

"Don't get any ideas, doc, the hospital said I was weird, not crazy."

Priest chuckled and leaned into Lucky's body as he slipped a lean arm across his shoulders.

"Have you tried medication?"

"That's for people that don't embrace their crazy. Insanity is such a weird concept. Normal people get all kinds of weird ideas. A person doesn't fit some mold, and all of sudden, people in the white coats wants to lock them up. Shameful."

"What about Matt? Do you think he's crazy?"

"Hell no, he smart, handsome, cute as fuck when he gets all stuttering when someone flirts with him. Oh, and don't forget funny and a great cuddler."

"Cuddler?"

Priest cringed as he looked down and suddenly found the frayed knee of his jeans fascinating. It was one subject he'd never brought up with Dr. Campbell. He always felt it would bring up questions he wasn't ready to answer.

"Yeah, he curls up with me most nights, except for the last two nights and I called his ass on that bullshit. Besides, when he sleeps with me, it's like having my own electric blanket. Dude loves to sleep on top, and he must have some really vivid dreams." Lucky suggestively waggled his brows.

He rolled his eyes and elbowed his friend in the ribs. "Lucky, really, you have to bring that up?"

"Yeah, she asked a question, I warned her. And you know me, you should already know better."

"He doesn't appear to have intimacy issues with you, then why the Touch workshop?"

"Oh, we don't have that kind of intimacy, but a man would be a eunuch not to be tempted. Because all that furry skin makes a man's mouth water, but that's not the point."

That was definitely the point. His ex had always made him wax—everything. Stubble covered cheeks weren't acceptable. No one in his life ever told him that he made their mouth water. Priest couldn't take his eyes off Lucky even when he continued as if he didn't shock the hell out of him.

"Priest flinches when people get too close, closes down when someone starts to flirt with him. I just thought they'd be able to help him get over whatever aversion he has to touch."

"You'd be his partner at these sessions, right?"

"Yeah, no one else is gonna do it. They won't understand Priest doesn't like something and I won't let some fucker scare my pretty bear. So, what do you say, Doc, do you think it'll help or hurt?"

"If Matt is agreeable I don't see a problem with him attending the workshop, but if he has any issues—bad feelings then he should leave. He's been forced—"

"Stop right there, doc, I'd never force Priest into anything. I may have only recently discovered why he has problems with intimacy, but I suspected. Those men are in his past and will stay there. Unless Priest wants to give me details, I don't need to know."

"But what about your radical honesty philosophy?"

"This isn't about honesty, it's about comfort and safety. When or if he ever feels safe enough to share—"

"Lucky, I've always felt safe with you."

Lucky shrugged his shoulders and went silent, that was unnatural for him.

"Why don't I talk to Matt alone for the rest of the session?"

Lucky nodded and then leaned over to kiss Priest on the mouth. "You want me to wait around?"

"No, you can go ahead. You'll be bouncing around the waiting room and making the receptionist nervous."

"Yeah, yeah, nice to meet you, Doc."

"You as well, Lucky."

Priest couldn't take his gaze off Lucky as the man stood to exit the office. The soft click of the door deafening in the silence. With Lucky's departure, the peace he felt disappeared and the always present panic which existed at the back of his brain began to build.

"Why haven't you ever mentioned Lucky or the sleeping arrangements before?"

He turned back to her, turned the questions over in his mind searching for the right answer, and the only one he could come up with he couldn't voice—he was in love with weird and accident-prone Lucky Trenton. And the possibility of what he wanted frightened him.

5 LET'S CUDDLE THE FUCK OUTTA EACH OTHER

Priest was pushed up tight behind him on Lucky's motorcycle as they pulled up to the commune where the workshop was being held. He noticed Priest became tenser the closer they got, and Priest's hands were knotted in the front of his t-shirt. This wasn't about making his bear more nervous. He pulled to a stop in front the building marked office and cut the engine.

"Do you want to go," Lucky asked. "We can head home, and you can pick a movie, even one of those sappy movies you like. I'll hate it, but for you, I'd suffer through it."

"Don't you ever lie?"

He ignored the question. "So, what's it gonna be?"

"You won't leave me alone, right?"

"No, I'll be there every fucking second until you get sick of me."

"I don't think that would ever happen."

"Let's go get checked in. I sprung for one of those fancy private cabins. I know how you love your bubble baths. Which I think is totally weird, but whatever."

Priest pushed at his shoulders, and Lucky patted his broad, muscled thigh to get him moving. The other man swung off and stood beside Lucky's bike. He removed his half helmet as Priest did the same. He didn't tell Priest he'd signed them up as a couple to do private sessions except for the first day of meet and greet shit.

He dismounted and grabbed Priest's hand to tug him toward the office. Chimes rang as he opened the door. A graying woman with a kind face wearing a long, flowing dress greeted them.

"Good afternoon, Gentlemen."

He snorted, and it earned him an elbow to the ribs. "Don't abuse the love of your life."

"Behave, at least until we get checked in."

"Fine." He huffed and turned back to the lady. "I'm Lee Trenton."

"Mr. Trenton, I'm Laurie, whatever you require just let me know."

"Thanks. My man is demanding as—"

"Lucky, we're among strangers, watch your language."

"Why I adore you baffles me."

"Have you two been together long?"

"Two years," Lucky answered, and it earned him a grunt from Priest. He may be weird, but he'd known what he wanted since he'd hugged Priest the first time.

"Your cabin is already. Just sign these forms, and I'll run your card."

He reached back and pulled his wallet from his pocket, he opened it to remove his card. Sliding it across the counter, he reached for a pen to sign the papers.

"Here's the itinerary for the weekend with couple and group activities. Tonight, you'll get settled in, tomorrow morning after breakfast there's a group activity where introductions are made, and you'll share what brought you here. It's not required to give your reasons, but introductions are, and the coordinator will explain the rules."

"What about dinner?"

"You can either order room service or join everyone in the communal cabin."

"Thanks."

"Once you pull out, you'll take a left, and you're in cabin 12. It's the most private one, just as you requested."

"Requested," Priest asked.

"We'll talk it about when we get settled."

"Yes, we're going to."

Oh, he didn't like that fucking tone. It's the one Priest used when he thought Lucky did something wrong. Fifteen minutes and he was already in fucking trouble. Great.

They exited the office, hopped back on the bike and drove toward their cabin. It was one large room with a small fridge, sink and counter with a coffee maker under three cabinets. There was one bed, a sitting area, no T.V., but they'd each brought their laptops. He laid their backpacks on the bed.

"What did you tell them?"

"What do you mean?"

"You know what I mean."

"Fuck, okay, we're here as boyfriends. I knew you would get all freaked out about other people touching you. We're gonna work on intimacy, but there won't be no fucking involved. Maybe if ya want to take a chance on a cuddle puddle thing, then we'll do it. If ya don't like any of this shit, we'll check out and head the hell home."

"You don't have problems with touching and sex."

He couldn't interpret Priest's tone, he thought he heard wistfulness. His obsession with observing Priest over the years and anticipating his needs and moods made him an expert on his man. It was just a matter of patience.

"But you do, and people need touch, not so much sex. Fucking is mostly about getting off. Making love is completely different. This weekend isn't about that. Touch is really fucking important." He'd grown up in a house where affection was a natural thing. Lucky couldn't imagine the life Priest led without touch or love, but worse the touch of others that made him fearful years later.

"You're obsessed with sex."

Lucky watched Priest dig through his bag for his e-reader and set it on the nightstand. He knew talk of sex made Priest uncomfortable. He'd be lying if he didn't want Priest under, on top or on his hands and knees, but he didn't want fucking with Priest. Maybe one day they'd get down and dirty. His goal, for now, was to get his bear used to more than the innocent touches.

"Man, getting off is fucking amazing. Doesn't matter if it's by hand, mouth or a tight ass, it's a transcendent experience. That look in your man's eyes the first time you push in, the way his mouth falls open a bit on a moan and his pupils become blown, nothing fucking like it."

"I don't need to know about you and sex with other—" Priest's cheeks were flaming red above his ginger beard.

"What's wrong?"

"Nothing." Priest's voice cracked, and Lucky knew the man was lying.

"Cut the fucking bullshit. We don't lie to each other—ever. You save that shit for everyone else. Don't fucking insult me."

Wide, green eyes turned toward him with a hint of hurt shining in them, but Lucky turned away and ripped his shirt over his head throwing it over his backpack. Guilt wasn't something he was used to, hell, he didn't think he'd ever felt it before. He knew fucking well he'd never raised his voice to Priest. His bear was too sweet.

"I need to make a phone call to let Ma know we got here." He strode quickly toward the door then rushed outside pulling his phone out as he went.

Lucky pressed the speed dial for his parents' phone.

"You fucked up didn't you?"

"Ma, don't start, where's Dad?"

"Put our least fucked up child on speaker."

He snorted at his dad's voice.

"Okay, we're both here, what did you do?"

"I fucking yelled at him."

"What could Priest do to make you yell at him. That would be like kicking a puppy," Lily screeching in his ear wasn't helping his mood.

"He lied to me."

"Son, not everyone was raised to open their mouth and verbally vomit every thought in their head."

"But he's never blatantly fucking lied to me before."

"Okay, let's think rationally for a moment, what happened before he allegedly—"

"There's no fucking alleged about it."

"Fine, what did you do?"

"Why is this always my fucking fault?"

"We're off topic, son, your mother's just trying to be understanding."

"She's not helping!" And again he raised his voice. Another bad habit he didn't need.

"Go to the bathroom and jerk one out because you're tenser than a virgin in a Viagra factory."

"What the fuck does that even mean?"

"It means abstinence is unnatural for Lee Eros Trenton."

"Motherfucker, can we not use my full name?"

"As far as I know, I don't fuck Mothers that would be your father's job."

"Can we get off the topic of my parents fucking or who they fuck and my lack of coitus with my pretty bear and get back on fucking topic?"

"Coitus." Lily snorted and giggled like a dirty-minded teen boy.

"Why did I call you two to help me? Please fucking enlighten me."

"Because all your friends think you're an asshole and want to murder you in your sleep?"

"I'm hanging the fuck up because you're being mean," Lucky pouted as he listened to Lily's laugh at his expense.

"Lily, go relax, let me talk to Lucky."

"He's being sensitive."

He listened to her huff, but then it went quiet.

"Son, what have we talked about?"

"Don't bait the evil one in training."

"No," Damon chuckled. "And don't let her hear you say that."

"Why not? It's true."

"No, it's not. We've talked about you having a softer approach with Priest. His treatment was unconscionable. You yelling at him isn't going to help. You've attuned yourself to his every mood since the moment you met him.

How do you think he felt when you treated him like you did?"

"You made your point. I'm an asshole."

"You're not an asshole, son, we raised you to be too honest and sometimes that comes off as being a dick. Priest knows you probably better than anyone else, but despite his gorgeous body—"

"Quit thinking about my man's body."

Damon continued like Lucky hadn't spoken, "And handsome face, he's vulnerable and fragile, and how do we treat vulnerable partners?"

"With the utmost respect and love as we foster a feeling of self-worth and safety."

"Exactly, now get your hippie ass back to Priest and make it up to your man or I may revisit the option of an open relationship so that I can take care of him."

"And I'll tell Ma you tried to sleep with her sister."

"Please, I already told your mother that, they're identical twins. Besides, that's a threesome we won't mention."

"You're fucking sick, man, just sick, now, I'll never be able to look at Aunt Rose again."

"Then don't make threats you have no chance of carrying through with. Besides, it sounded more enjoyable than it was."

He disconnected the call without a word. Maybe talking to Priest's shrink wasn't a bad idea. He knew he wasn't normal, he could get some meds and then heavily dose his family. Lucky shoved his phone into his pocket and took a calming breath before walking back inside. Priest was perched on the edge of the bed with his hands twisted on his lap.

"I'm sorry. I'm an asshole."

"You've never gotten mad at me before."

Lucky approached the bed and sat down next to Priest. He tried not to frown when Priest leaned away. Priest never shied away from his touch. "I wasn't mad, just frustrated. You never lie to me. I thought we were passed that shit."

"I didn't lie, it really was nothing. Where did you go?"

"I went to call Ma and Dad."

"Why?"

"Because I yelled at you."

"And," Priest asked.

"They implied I was an asshole who needs to treat you with the utmost respect to show you your self-worth and make sure you always feel safe."

"Is that what you believe?"

"Of course, you ain't perfect, but you're damn close."

"Smooth, Trenton, really smooth."

"I try. You want me to run you a bath so you can relax while I order dinner?"

"You don't have to—"

"I got this shit, I know just how you like it. I gotta make up for being a bastard. I have to take care of my bear, right? I rhymed…it was like poetry or some shit."

"Go away."

"Ma was already fucking mean to me, don't you start." Lucky leaned in and gave Priest a quick kiss, then bounced off the bed and headed for the bathroom grabbing the bottle of Priest's bubble bath. He thought it was cute how much Priest loved his baths. It was sort of his happy place at the end of the day.

Tomorrow was soon enough to get into the deep shit. For tonight, it would just be Priest and him. At least he knew Priest would sleep next to him. It was the only thing he'd fucking had for the last two years, but he fucking hoped their weekend would change something even if it didn't make his pretty bear see him as more than his best friend. It was more important Priest found himself and his safety.

6 THAT'S NEW

The scents of a familiar incense he recognized as one of Lucky's favorites filled the large room. There was a circle of cushions littered around the room. The door had a sign that said Couple's Workshop. Priest already sat through the introductions and the rules, they were also informed of a cuddle group later that evening. He watched couples filing in, mostly straight, but a few lesbian, so it appeared Lucky and him were the only male couple.

"Good afternoon, everyone, how is everyone today?" A perky woman who looked like she was going to a Yoga class skipped into the room. That was way too much.

Everyone responded, but he was frozen until he felt Lucky's arms twine around his waist from behind. Soft lips surrounded by stubble teased the side of his throat and his eyes closed. Almost three years of sleeping beside Lucky most nights, all the touches and caring gestures hadn't prepared him for this.

"I'm Carmen, please find a cushion, one of you will sit cross legged. Your partner will sit on your lap facing you with their legs around your waist, the soles of their feet together and arms over your shoulders."

"Yes or no, Priest, this is your decision."

He could only nod and let Lucky lead him to the back of the room. Lucky sat down and crossed his legs, then held his hand out for him. His body shook slightly as he straddled Lucky's lap and eased down until his ass was cradled between Lucky's thighs. It was the most intimate position he'd ever experience with Lucky or anyone else. He shifted uncomfortably at the strangeness.

"To start, we're just going to focus on breathing," Carmen's voice was soft. "Close your eyes. Focus on your partner's breathing. Matching your breaths to theirs. Inhale when your partner exhales."

Lucky's clear blue eyes focused on his, and his fingers tenderly stroked the small of his lower back. Music with a lot of chimes softly played.

"You're holding your fucking breath," Lucky whispered. "And close your eyes."

He exhaled heavily and tried to do as directed. They both wore pajama bottoms and t-shirts, but he was hyper aware of Lucky's warmth where their skin connected. He peeked at Lucky and studied the handsome angles of his face. The dark blond brows with one bisected with a scar from one of Lucky's many accidents and the other pierced with a small stainless steel hoop. His cheekbones were high, up close you could count the cute freckles that slashed across his cheeks and nose. A slender nose that was slightly bent with a bump at the bridge. Lucky's lips were wide and thin, but the bottom one had a nibble-worthy pout. He was so beautiful, and Priest didn't understand why Lucky treated him like he was special.

Years of gentle touches, Lucky made sure he was always comfortable and cared for, hell, sometimes Lucky even made sure Priest ate before he did. Lucky would watch him as Priest would eat with this odd expression in his eyes—almost like satisfaction. Then something tickled at the back of his mind and he suddenly realized he'd seen that look before, it was the way Damon watched and cared for Lily. He'd witnessed Damon making Lily a plate before he even attempted to get his own.

He'd always found it stupid to be jealous of the relationship Lily and Damon had. There was no mistaking the love they had for each other—even with the oddness of their partnership. Now, he didn't get the radical honesty, he couldn't imagine Lucky coming home to say he'd been checking out and flirting with someone else, maybe even having sex with another person. He felt his brow furrow at the thought of Lucky with anyone. Priest wasn't stupid enough to think extraordinarily handsome Lucky went without, but Priest didn't want to think about it.

Soft lips brushed at the creases between his brows, and he opened his eyes all the way to find Lucky watching him. A half-smile quirking his mouth as he withdrew, but then Lucky rested his forehead to Priest's and flexed his arms pulling Priest closer. Priest stiffened to camouflage his shiver at the closeness.

That was new, although he'd noticed Lucky, the gorgeous, weird man caused him all kinds of strange emotions and thoughts over the years. The instructor's voice broke through his thoughts, but he didn't pay attention as he was too focus on the man holding him. It was familiar yet different.

"Today is about recapturing intimacy. Touch is such a simple act and conveys everything we feel. Make eye contact and with touch let your partner know how you feel about them. There's no rush. Find your safety and comfort."

He caught the end of one of Lucky's locs and rubbed it between his fingertips, the texture course, but strangely soft. Suddenly Lucky's dreads fell and caressed over his skin. Calloused fingers traced his arms from shoulders to his hands, Lucky wrapped his hands around his wrists and pulled Priest's hands around to rest on Lucky's lean pecs. Lucky trapped one over his heart and Priest spread his fingers. His stomach twisted and tightened, heat began to build.

"Don't panic, I can tell when you start to lose your shit."

"I'm not panicking." It was the truth, well, not in the sense of his normal panic attacks. His breaths were sharp coming in quick pants, but he didn't feel like there was a vice around his chest. The anxiousness which screamed for him to run wasn't there. To the contrary, Priest wanted to get closer.

He shifted his hips and sank deeper into the cradle of Lucky's legs. Lucky's chest rumbled under his hands. That was new, Priest experimentally rubbed his palms against Lucky's chest and felt the man's nipple rings catch. Lucky's hands settled on his sides and stroked along his ribs. He nibbled nervously at his lower lip. It took all his control not to squirm.

His gaze caught and held Lucky's as they touched. There wasn't anything remotely sexual about it and nothing they hadn't done countless times in the past. Safety is all he ever felt, there wasn't any pushing like with the other men he'd encountered. The terror his ex induced didn't come into play. Was this how it was supposed to be when you cared about someone?

Priest loved Lucky, had for a long time and it went beyond friends. He wasn't stupid enough not to recognize what his feelings were, but he couldn't take that step. Men wanted sex, and he knew he wasn't ready, probably never would be able to trust someone to that degree not even Lucky. He started to drop his chin, but fingertips pushed at his chin, and Lucky's forehead rested heavier to his. No words were exchanged, none needed to be, and he just let himself feel comfort while it lasted.

✦ ✦ ✦

"I'm so fucking bored," Lucky whined.

Priest laughed as he cuddled on the hammock outside their cabin while Lucky rocked them. His best friend needed constant chaos, or his brain started to short circuit.

"You can survive without Brawlers or your cartoons for another 24 hours."

"What if I can't? Who the fuck doesn't put TVs in a place like this or a bar?"

Lucky's disgusted tone was cute, his pouting even cuter. He wouldn't tell him that though. The man's ego was already at capacity. "This is sort of a couple's type place for them to rekindle their relationships. I can't believe you brought us to a couple's intimacy workshop."

"Don't give me fucking shit, I was trying to be nice, and you know how fucking hard that is for me. That old lady nearly lost her false teeth when I said fuck earlier at dinner."

He shifted to get more comfortable and brought them into impossibly closer contact. "Normal people don't use fuck as an exclamation point or have perfected the use of the word as a noun, verb and adjective."

"We've known each other four fucking years, man, don't you know I ain't fucking normal yet?"

"I couldn't imagine you normal."

"It's insulting that you'd even have the thought."

"Lucky, thank you for this."

"What're you thanking me for, man?"

"I don't know, it was nice to be touched."

"Baby, I always touch you."

It wasn't the first time Lucky used endearments, but it was mostly Lucky calling him his bear. "I know, but this just seemed different."

"Different," Lucky asked.

He settled his head over Lucky's heart and listened to the familiar rhythm of it. The sound had been his lullaby by years now. "I wasn't panicky and waiting for a hit or to be held down. It wasn't always like that, sometimes it started off gentle, but when my flight response would ease that's when he'd strike."

"I don't want to sound like an asshole, but why'd you stay?"

"You get used to not being wanted. My Mom, well, she just saw me as a mistake and a disappointment. Dad didn't give a shit at all as long as I had good grades and excelled at sports. I hated sports."

"Yeah, you're not the most athletic type."

At the words, he tried to suck in his stomach.

"Cut that bullshit out, I like that you're cuddly. My own personally teddy bear."

"Asshole."

"Again, that's not fucking news."

"We'd dated for six months, and he was super sweet when he asked me to spend that first night I didn't hesitate. I was stupid. I should have run, but he kept me that whole weekend and—"

"You don't have to explain." Lucky kissed the top of his head. "You were terrified, but you don't have to be anymore."

"I know, you remember the day we met?"

"Oh man, you were so fucking hot."

"You're such a liar."

"I'm incapable of lying remember? My parents damaged my brain at an early age. You were wearing a gray v-neck t-shirt, baggy jeans and black boots. Your beard was just starting to grow in. I thought you were going to puke you were so fucking nervous."

"Everyone else nodded or shook my hands, you though—"

"I couldn't resist just one hug, and I told you we were going to be best friends."

"You were so weird."

"But you found me irresistible."

"I wouldn't go that far." He chuckled as Lucky squeezed him tight. Priest closed his eyes and absorbed Lucky's warmth. The man ran hot. He was emotionally worn out from the day and all the weird thoughts it caused. Priest felt himself start to drift but tried to make himself get up.

"Get some sleep, pretty bear. We'll go inside later."

He didn't say a word as he relaxed and at the edge of his mind, he swore he heard Lucky softly talking as if to lull him to sleep. Priest couldn't understand what he was saying as he drifted off safe with Lucky.

7 BABYSITTER LUCKY: THE COOL UNCLE

Cartoons blared as he sat sandwiched between Princess and Juvie shoveling in cereal and starting an impressive juice box pyramid. Lucky loved sleepovers with his nieces. It gave Brody and Trouble a night to themselves with him watching Princess. Juvie was a new addition to the crew, Elijah, Tank and Scary adopted her about six months before. She was a smart-assed little shit, and Lucky adored her.

He was the coolest fucking Uncle, they both told him so, not in those words. The dreads and beads were as far as they would let him corrupt the brats, cussing would get him fucking grounded from Niece Time.

"We're going to get Uncle Priest presents today?"

"What we getting him?"

"You'll see, I ain't tell ya because y'all snitched me out last time."

"Aw, Luck, he hated that last thing ya bought him. That teddy bear was bigger than he was. We dragged that thing through the store for nothing."

"He loves that fu—it."

"Uncle Lucky, you tied it to the motorcycle. We almost got pulled over. If they hadn't been laughing so hard. You had us in the sidecar, and a Priest sized bear on the bit—back seat."

"Watch your language. We were grounded the last time, Juvie. Scary and Tank nearly kicked my butt, if they weren't old and tired out before they got to me I woulda been dead, man, dead."

"You have to get Uncle Priest something nice. Like Papa gets Daddy."

"I get Priest nice things."

"Luck, man, you gotta have some game, do something romantic like. Take him on dates like Dad and Papa take Daddy. They get all dressed up like they're going to funerals. Daddy is always smiling when he comes home."

"I'm sure he is." Those three were freaks, he was surprised his niece wasn't traumatized. He never came over unannounced anymore. Bodies aren't supposed to bend like that—poor, poor Elijah. Ropes and shit, what was wrong with a good old-fashioned—he banished the thoughts before his cereal rebelled and tried to come back up.

"I'm just saying—" Juvie pouted and went back to shoveling cereal into her mouth like it was going to be taken away.

She'd gotten better since she'd joined the crew, but six months wasn't long enough to make the little girl feel like she completely belonged. The pre-teen hadn't had the best start in life, but Elijah, Tank and Scary were doing a fucking amazing job with her.

"We gotta take the car today."

"Aw, man, your car smells like feet."

"I'll have you know that car is a classic."

"A classic piece of crap."

Lucky gasped and grabbed his chest, milk sloshed onto his Grateful Dead shirt. His 68 *Nova SS* was the shit, they didn't know what the fuck they were talking about. His baby was a classic.

"Can we bring air freshener," Princess asked.

The little traitor, he'd expect it from Juvie, but not his sweet and loving Princess.

"I'm withholding Dots."

"Oh no, don't threaten the Dots, man," Juvie pointed a finger at him. "Don't be that Uncle, Lucky, don't be that Uncle. You're losing coolest points, Crave's gaining."

"Don't threaten me! Crave will never take my spot—never!"

"Fine, don't got to be all dramatic about it." Juvie shook her head, and her dreads with the rainbow wraps tinkled with the tiny bells that were woven into them.

He'd spent hours on her hair. "Okay, I laid out clothes for y'all, nothing your parents sent. I won't be embarrassed today."

They jumped from the couch, set their bowls down and took off running. Juvie wouldn't wear a dress to save her life, but he'd made her a hippie peasant blouse and thin-soled sandals with more bells in the hemp rope. Princess got a skirt in a beautiful Indian print with mirrors embroidered into the design and a white blouse, along with the same sandals only a few sizes smaller than Juvie's.

Brody and Trouble took over the guest house out back. It wasn't much but perfect for a small family of three. They weren't there, Tank's old cabin turned into the couple's getaway spot. Normally it was where Scary and Tank took Elijah, but they'd headed off to some secret locale to get freaky for the weekend.

Priest normally supervised, but the cupboards were empty, so he was volunteered to run all the errands today. Zerk and Landon were running the shop. Lucky pushed to his feet, gathered up the bowls and the juice boxes, then he headed to get dressed. He'd called the Animal Shelter earlier, they'd gotten in a litter of kittens, munchkins. Priest always said he wanted a cat, but the times Lucky brought up going to get one, Priest said no.

Lucky talked it over with the guys, and everyone was fine with Lucky getting Priest one. Herc was already good with cats. The weird ass dog tried to friend the neighborhood ones and earned scratches as a reward for his friendliness. It was all planned. Plus, a little something extra. He just hoped he didn't fuck up and get Priest something he didn't want. He always tried to get Priest little things, just like Damon did for Lily. He just hoped Priest didn't put all that shit together. He didn't seem like the courting type, but he wanted to be—for Priest.

◆ ◆ ◆

"Don't squeeze the crap out of her before we get her home to Priest." he told Princess as she carried the yet unnamed new member of the crew in a sling he'd made from a tie-dyed scarf he had in the car. The kitten had its head poked out, but the rest of her was hidden.

"Lucky, you got him a three-legged, one-eyed cat, it's broken."

"It's not broken, she wouldn't have been adopted. It's not cute enough. Just push the cart."

"Fine, but it's still broken."

"We gotta get all the things she needs." He herded his nieces down the cat aisle ignoring the strange looks he received from the other customers. They always looked at Juvie and Princess, then back at him. It's like he kidnapped the heathens. Juvie's locs started to fall from the twist he'd put them in. He stopped her and fixed them.

"You have cute kids." A woman probably about his age smiled at him.

Oh man, a flirty woman, he'd never handled those well. Also, it wasn't polite to bellow I'm gay and take off running. There were times and places for honesty, and he didn't think now was one of them.

"Oh, no, not mine, nieces. Juvie and Princess." Okay, maybe he should have not announced their nicknames.

"We picked out his boyfriend a kitten, see." Princess pointed to the kitten.

He rolled his eyes as the woman stared at the kitten.

"She wasn't going to be adoptable. My bear will love her."

"We hope, he wasn't crazy about the man-sized teddy bear we got last time."

"He loved that bear too."

"Relax, Lucky, that vein in your forehead popped out. It's gross."

"Why did I bring you with me?"

"Because we were released into your care and we're not old enough to stay home to take care of ourselves."

"Right, right." Lucky darted a glance at the stranger and found her smiling. "Is it too late to say I don't know them?"

"I think so."

"Fu—" He brought his hand up and pushed at his closed lids with his thumb and index finger.

"Language, remember, we don't want to be grounded again. Uncle Zerk doesn't put extra sugar on our cereal when he watches us."

"Come on, we have to get stuff for the new crew member and have to look at one more thing before we leave."

"It was nice meeting you and you have a great kitten."

"Thanks," he muttered and ushered the girls along, throwing stuff in the cart as they went. He didn't realize how much stuff a small puff of fur needed. They made it to a large glass case. He glanced at the kitten and saw her watching the rats scurry around the enclosure.

"Are we getting her a snack," Juvie asked as she leaned against his right leg and Princess mirrored on the left side.

"No, we're getting her a best friend."

"You're getting Priest a one-eyed, three-legged kitten with a rat for a best friend?"

"Yeah, why?"

"You give the worst gifts." Princess shook her head as she scratched the kitten's folded down ears.

His girls were shitting on his plan.

"Shush it, my pretty bear will love them."

"You keep saying that, Luck, but—" She opened her arms motioning to the cat and rat.

"Don't, I'm doing this."

"Fine, but he's going to say he loves it and then—"

"He'll love it, I know it."

"You can cuddle with us when you're crying."

He tracked down a salesperson, finished filling the cart with the items he needed for the rat, Juvie carried the cardboard box with holes with the kitten's best friend. This was going to great, it had to be, he couldn't keep fucking up this courting.

An hour later after a lunch of Vegan food. These kids were weird, and it wasn't all his fault. "Priest," he called out for Priest, the girls close on his heels.

"Hey, they live." Priest chuckled as he appeared from the kitchen.

"You're not funny. It was a close one. They've been nightmares."

"Couldn't be that bad. Did you feed them?"

"Yes, we had cereal and juice boxes for breakfast while we watched cartoons, then we had vegan for lunch."

"And you survived?"

"You're being a smart ass today, and I don't fu—I don't like it."

"I'm sorry."

"No, you're not. Girls, we returning his presents."

"Presents?"

"Don't get too excited, Uncle Priest. It's like the teddy bear again."

"I loved my teddy bear."

"See!" He looked down to glare at one girl then the other.

"What did you get me?"

He reached out and took Priest's hand leading him toward the couch. "I know you always say no, but I wanted to do it." Stepping behind Priest, he wrapped his arms around his waist. "You've gotta name them though."

"Oh, Lucky, I—"

"We should have went with jewelry or dinner."

"You don't like them?" He dropped his forehead to Priest's shoulder.

"They're perfect." Priest spun in his arms.

The thick arms tightening around him drove the oxygen from his lungs.

"They're so weird, let's go watch TV in Lucky's room."

"Don't touch my stuff."

"Not without germ stuff."

"She hates me."

"Juvie loves you. Can I take them out of their carrier?"

"They're yours, do what you want. Um, the kitten isn't really…"

"Isn't what?"

"No one was taking her, all her litter mates got adopted, but she was left."

"Why?"

"You'll see."

Priest released him and nearly jogged around the couch to drop to his knees next the carrier. The kitten and rat both had their faces pressed to the door. "I can't believe you got me and cat and a rat."

"I like the dichotomy of it."

"You would."

He watched Priest release the latch and open the door. Priest reached in and removed the kitten first. He held his breath as he waited for a reaction.

"She's beautiful," Priest whispered as he nuzzled the kitten's head.

"I know she's missing a leg and an eye, but she didn't deserve—"

"They're perfect, Lucky, really."

Priest's face and eyes were lit up with a smile. The man had the kitten and rat tucked under his chin.

"She gets around pretty good. Hobbles a bit."

"Born like this?"

"When they found the litter, she had a wound on her leg, and it couldn't be saved, same with her eye."

"We have so much to get."

"Already taken care of, me and the girls went shopping after the animal shelter. I had to pick up the rat too. All you've got to do is pick names."

"What should I name them?"

"That's all on you, I picked them, you name them."

"I gotta think about it." Priest rose to his feet and approached him, the pretty man had his new pets cuddled against his chest. "Thank you, Lucky."

Soft lips had brushed his before Priest stepped back with his cheeks a bit red above his beard.

"You're welcome."

It was the first time Priest ever kissed him first. Normally it was just a quick peck to tease Priest, and he always put plenty of space between them afterward so that Priest wouldn't feel crowded. His parents were odd, but they loved each other unconditionally, always had, and part of him wanted exactly what they had. Well, not exactly, he wasn't sharing Priest—his bear was all his.

"Let's get them settled in. Will they sleep with us?"

He felt his lips tug into a wide smile at the question. Priest had slept with him every night for the past two weeks since they'd returned from the workshop.

"The kitten for sure, but the rat's gonna have to stay in his cage."

"Probably, don't want to lose him somewhere in the house. Herc's going to be so excited to have friends. I have to introduce them." Priest took off calling Herc's name.

He'd made his pretty bear happy, and it couldn't get much fucking better than that.

8 THEIR FUR BABIES WERE AS WEIRD AS THEIR OTHER DADDY

Priest heard the doorbell ring. No one showed that early in the day. It was considered a capital offense. He peeked around the corner to catch sight of Lucky as he threw open the door and bestowed the unwelcome guests with the sign of the cross. "Be gone, evil ones," he shouted as he tried to kick the door closed but Lou rolled her eyes and kicked the door right back open.

"What the fuck is wrong with you," Leigh-Lou demanded as she entered with Linus on her heels.

Lucky threw his hands up in defeat. "Please come in, we didn't have anything better to do today."

Priest couldn't help laughing. The three Trenton siblings getting together could end two ways. One, was they completely tortured an unsuspecting victim. The other option, found them passed out from drinking to ignore each other. Either was always perversely amusing. Well, as long as he wasn't the victim or there wasn't puke.

"What did I do now, I haven't even left the fucking house today."

"Does the occasion call for alcohol or something stronger," Priest asked as he stepped into the foyer.

"You're not funny, Bear, get rid of them."

"I'm not throwing your siblings out, play nice." He rolled his eyes and disappeared, but the volume at which they spoke could be heard down the block.

He didn't consider it eavesdropping when they weren't exactly hiding their conversation. Looking toward Herc's huge bed set up in the corner of the kitchen, he found the Mastiff curled up with his new friends, the kitten's body was tucked under his chin, and the rat was on top of his head. It was weird the three of them were rarely apart.

"So, what is it now?"

"You gave the parents grandkids, granted they're of the furry variety, but since it's you, they consider you getting pets with your man as a marriage proposal." Lou's voice was filled with disgust.

Priest would've freaked if he didn't know them so well. Lily wanted to marry all her kids off even if she despised the ones they brought home. Luckily Lily liked him even if he was just Lucky's best friend.

"What the fuck, this is about Cyclops and Plague?"

"You named them Cyclops and Plague," Linus asked as his voice rose a few octaves.

"Yeah, Priest was going to name them something all cute and shit, I called veto."

He groaned and opened the fridge, he wasn't going to name them something cute, but he hadn't had time to choose before Lucky picked the most inappropriate names. He grabbed three beers and carried them to the living room finding Lou laid out on the couch with her arm over her eyes with her feet in Linus' lap.

"How you get that man to put up with you fucking amazes me."

Lou's opinion wasn't new. She'd pulled him aside plenty of times to warn him to run hard and fast from Lucky. Sometimes he didn't know if she was joking.

"He loves me."

"Don't start, Lucky." He spent all his time admonishing his best friend for one thing or another.

"I swear he's more warped than you."

Lucky glared at Lou but snapped his teeth shut when Priest started to hand out bottles.

"The natives finished off the whiskey last night," Priest informed them. He was still cleaning up the kitchen from the midnight experiment. He didn't even want to know what they attempted to eat.

All he knew was he woke up with a softly snoring Lucky with his face hidden in the crook of Priest's shoulder—a very naked Lucky. He'd seen Lucky naked plenty of times and his best friend had no shame in his body. Normally he avoided letting his eyes travel below Lucky's chest, but a very perked up part of Lucky's anatomy nudged his bare thigh insistently. He couldn't really analyze what went through his head, and he really didn't want to examine it too closely.

"Ma's lined up suitable breeding stock, and we're supposed to meet with the egg and sperm donors. I am not being a womb for the cause, Linus can take one for the team."

"She swears he's adopted, so she'll want you to grunt out a kid."

"I'm not doing it, Lucky."

71

Priest took a seat on the arm of Lucky's seat and squeaked as he was pulled down onto the man's lap.

"Don't get all fucking cutesy couple bullshit with us. You're off the fucking hook. You got a fucking man. I don't want one. Can you imagine me putting up with some cock with legs long enough to get the egg dividing into some parasite that'll feed off me for ten fucking months? Motherfucker, that's like some alien shit, can't they just grow them in vats and I can visit it until it's ready to slime its way into this fucked up world. We're dealing with overpopulation now."

Priest snorted, no one could accuse Lou of being maternal. He still remembered the night she'd drunkenly poured herself out of the back of a cab after witnessing what she described as the horror of birth. She'd just kept repeating that it wasn't done, put it back. Lou had slept on the cool tile of the bathroom floor that night. He didn't think he'd handle it any better than her.

"It comes out with all this chunky slime, and they sometimes shit on their way out, they shit and piss, you're essentially a bathroom. Who would do that to themselves?"

"Apparently not you, but I'm not reproducing." Linus pointed at them and sneered.

That's when Priest noticed Linus had all his jewelry in, the septum, brow and lip ring, he was worrying the hoop through his lip with his teeth. He could count on one hand the times he'd seen Linus with his piercings visible.

"It be easier for you, Linus, insert tab a into slot b until the baby juice flows, one of your little swimmers has to beat the others. Hell, maybe you'll luck out, and you're sterile."

"Uh uh, not happening, Lou, this one is all you. Besides, have you looked at our family tree, can you imagine the limp mass of infant fuckedupedness one of us would create? It would be a total freak show. We'd have to search it for 666, it would be an Omen baby. Classical music would begin playing as it took its first breath and the angels would weep in fear, and the Pope's little hat would go up in flames."

"Um, man, we're atheists, remember?"

"If one of us produced the bearer of the Apocalypse we'd be believers."

He just sat back listening to the quickly diminishing conversation. Lucky loved Princess and Juvie, he was perfect with kids, but he knew Lucky never wanted any of his own, it seemed the sentiment was held by all the Trenton siblings.

"Just get some fur babies, and Ma will be happy," Lucky suggested.

Priest noticed the slow circles Lucky was drawing on his thigh. He relaxed his bulk back against Lucky's chest, and Lucky moved onto rubbing his belly, pushing into the softness. Goosebumps started to work their way over his skin. That was so not fucking good. Since the workshop, something changed. He'd always been aware of Lucky, found him attractive, loved his affection, but he was starting to crave more. He didn't think he'd ever be ready for sex, at least penetration. Pain was all he'd experienced during sex.

He laced his fingers through Lucky's as his past started to come back, the memories pushing at the blocks he kept in place except for when he slept. Lucky tightened his grip and nuzzled the side of his neck. Once more he felt safe, but how long before the memories came back?

"You know she won't." Lou shot to a sitting position and chugged most of her beer. "She's on a fucking mission, literally, we're supposed to fuck to give her little hippie shells to warp with her—"

"Our childhood was weird, but it wasn't bad. It could've been so much fucking worse than being ostracized for the clothes we wore or our inability to tell a lie."

"Parents normally want grandkids, Lily isn't any different. She just has her own idea of how to get them."

"We don't wanna have kids," Lou and Linus whined as they fell back having tantrums to make a toddler proud.

"Tell her that, but maybe say you're just not ready, use the *someday* excuse."

"Ma is an instant gratification type of crazy. She's got grandkids on the brain, and she will not stop until she has them."

"Maybe have her spend more time with Princess and Juvie. They call her grandma, and she loves it."

"Give her surrogate sycophants to worship at her bare, henna tattooed feet?"

"Exactly, and Princess and Mina already love her. Maybe a grandma weekend would take some of the pressure off you."

"Can we borrow the kids?"

"They're not a cup of sugar, motherfuckers, ya gotta be more subtle about it. You suddenly show up with mini-humans, and she's gonna smell a con."

"Okay, I'm out of here, I've got a late appointment," Priest said.

"What me to come with?"

"No, it's fine, she's a regular, but she travels a lot, so we had to make special arrangements."

"Okay, but text me when ya get there and when you're headed back."

"Yes, dear." He stood and Lucky's hand connected with his ass. His eyes widened, and he turned to look down at Lucky. "I know you didn't just put your hand on me."

"I always put my hands on you, and you love it."

Lucky rubbed his hands over his ass, and he swatted them away. The three of them together made them even weirder which should be impossible.

"Oh, sweet fake baby Jesus, you two should just fuck and get it the fuck over with." Linus groaned.

He shot a look at the other man and found him actually smiling—a real one. "Have you been pinching Lily's stash?"

"He has been acting weird. I was wondering if our family history of insanity had finally warped his brain."

"I'm out," Priest started to leave, but Lucky grabbed the front of his shirt to pull him down.

"Text me or I'll fucking worry, you know that."

"Fine, I'll text you, do you need proof of life pics?"

"Would you be naked?"

He felt his lips twitch and Lucky's eyes lit up. He gave Lucky a quick kiss to the corner of his mouth before backing away to escape.

Lucky was fucking his head up, and he wasn't quite sure how to deal with it or react. It wasn't anything overt, Lucky's treatment of him hadn't changed. His best friend didn't touch him any more than usual, they slept in the same bed, but that wasn't rare even before their weekend.

It was more his reaction that changed. He'd pick it apart later, right now he needed to get to work. He grabbed his jacket from the hook by the back door, then headed for the front waving at the siblings as he went. Maybe he'd take a long ride after work to clear his head and figure out what the fuck was going on with him.

9 SOMETHING WAS WEIRD IN THE LAND OF TWIRLED

He squeezed his dreads in his left hand as he set the blow dryer aside and checked to make sure they were completely dry. After he'd assured himself they were, he gathered the heavy mass in his hands, leaving one loc loose, and twisted them atop his head securing them by tying them with the loose one. He used his hemp lotion on his arms and chest, then slipped on his Tibetan Prayer beads around his right wrist and the black faux leather cuff around his left.

Lucky looked in the mirror, but he wasn't checking his appearance. He didn't really give a shit about stuff like that—comfort was his thing. As long as he was comfortable, then he was happy. No, he was tracking Priest's movements. He paid higher rent for the master bedroom because it had a private bathroom where Priest liked to take his baths. Priest was moving around what had turned into their room over the last month. He loved having Priest close, but the guys were starting to give him shit. As long as they didn't turn their bullshit onto Priest he could take it—he'd lived with Lily for twenty years, he could hold his own with them.

Priest glanced around before he removed his shirt, pale skin that wasn't covered with ink was sprinkled with the sexiest fucking freckles. Ginger hair thickly covered Priest's chest and soft belly. The early afternoon sunlight coming through the open curtains glittered off tiny hoops through Priest's nipples. The reddish-brown disks always looked hard and begging to be bit.

He thumped his hardening dick. "Behave, that ain't for us," he hissed.

"Did you say something?"

"Just talking to myself."

"You sure you don't need an appointment with my shrink?"

"I'm perfectly normal, man." He pouted and walked back into the bedroom, Plague and Cyclops were curled up on the made bed. Priest couldn't seem to leave the bed unmade.

He fell onto mattress wearing nothing but his towel, he reached out and scratched Cyclops' folded down ears, she batted at his hand with her one front paw. He rubbed her silky black fur as Plague waddled over to get her own petting.

"Jealous, little shit, let your sister have some love."

Rat whiskers had tickled his forearm before the fat rat laid her body across his hand. Priest's laughter drew his attention, and he found Priest still standing there with his t-shirt in hand.

"You spoiled them already."

"This is your doing, they're your pets."

"Uh huh," Priest seemed to want to ask something.

"What," he prompted.

"Do you—"

"Do I what?"

"Am I attractive?"

"Don't be an idiot, you're fucking gorgeous."

"I'm not skinny, or you know have six or eight-pack abs like the rest of you."

"Zerk doesn't either. Why are you asking? You've never worried about that shit before." He didn't like it, maybe Priest was thinking it was maybe time to date. Lucky sure as fuck didn't know if he could handle that. Seeing someone else touch and kiss his pretty bear. For a pacifist, he had a temper, and it was worse when it came to protecting Priest.

"I don't know, it was just…I don't like when people pay too much attention to me. When men and women flirt it's like my brain shuts down, but no one has really hit on me lately."

"Then their fucking blind, because you're totally fucking hot."

"Thanks." Priest smiled, but it wasn't quite right.

He was about to ask, but then Priest's phone started ringing. Before Lucky could grab it like usual Priest picked it up from the edge of the bed. Priest put it on speaker.

"Hello."

"Is this Matthew Beall?" A male voice that sounded like he had a big thorny stick up his ass asked.

"This is Matthew."

"Mr. Beall, I'm Dean Banning, I'm your family attorney."

"Is everything—" Priest paused as he reached for Lucky's hand.

Lucky didn't hesitate to thread their fingers together and tug Priest down to lie beside him. Priest glared at him, and Lucky rolled his eyes. He saw his Bear putting on a brave face, but tears started to appear in his hazel eyes.

"I'm sorry to inform you that your mother passed away a few days ago. Mr. Beall asked me to call and inform you, to let you know that the funeral is in two days and the Will reading is the next day on Friday."

"I don't have—haven't had any contact with my family in four years. I would've thought I'd be left out of the Will, especially hers."

Lucky tightened his arms around Priest as he listened to the words quiver and felt him choke back a sob. Maybe a part of his Bear hoped his mother would come around one day even if it was just a simple phone call, it wasn't impossible. His own fucking father couldn't be bothered to make the call.

"As per her wishes, you are to attend the reading."

"I don't know—"

"We'll be there." Lucky disconnected the call and wrapped the now sobbing Priest in his arms to tuck Priest tight to his bare chest. Tears dampened his skin, and he didn't care, he held tight as Priest's blunt nails dug into his pecs. He ignored the slight pain and awareness that alone proved he was a bastard.

"She's going to humiliate me. Even from the grave, she wants to punish me. What did I do wrong?"

"Nothing, baby, we can call him back say fuck her, we ain't coming. We'll go on the same as we've done the last four years. With you completely adoring me and lusting after my manly frame and hairy ass."

Priest's thick body shook as he laughed. He slipped his left arm between them, Priest's soft chest hair teased his palm as stroked upward until he used his fingertips to tilt Priest's head back. Their mouths were so close, just a few inches was all he had to lean down—he mentally shook off the urge.

"But seriously, you don't have to go."

"I should at least to say goodbye and see mydDad, there was a lot—"

"Okay, then that's what we'll do. I'm going to go talk to the guys, arrange for them to babysit." Priest started to shake his head. "Your babies will be fine for a few days."

"They'll develop abandonment issues."

"Plague and Cyclops will be fine, we'll be back before they even know we're gone."

"Fine, but if they start to rebel, it's all your fault."

"I'll be the bad parent." He leaned in and kissed Priest's wet lashes, the thick fringe tickled his lips. "Get my laptop, my wallet is on the dresser, buy us a couple tickets for tomorrow. Afterward, we'll go find us some fancy clothes to wear."

"I'm going to have to buy a suit and look awkward as hell, you'll get some flowing, natural fabric outfit and look like a million fucking bucks."

"Can't help how sexy I am."

"Has anyone ever told you your ego is out of control?"

"No, I've been told I'm quite humble."

Priest pushed him, and he rolled to his back, a breeze from the open window blew across his now completely bare body. He rarely covered himself when Priest was around, and he wouldn't call attention to it. Tightening his abs, he curled upward and stood, grabbing his cotton sleep pants from the end of the bed. He lifted one leg than the other pulling them up as he walked out of the bedroom.

The TV played loudly in the living room, Gib and Peaches opened today, and it was one of the rare days no one had an appointment scheduled. So, everyone would head in later just to hang out and wait for walk-ins.

Zerk and Trouble were the only ones who appeared to be home, Brody and Landon were at work. Scary was probably at Brawlers with Tank pining away for their man Elijah while he was working in Atlanta for the day.

"We need you to babysit."

"Finally going to get some, just lock them outside until you're done."

"Shut up, Zerk, Priest's mom died, so we're going to the funeral."

"Is Priest okay, he's never talked about his family."

"They didn't separate on the best of terms."

"When's the funeral, maybe we can all—"

He shook his head at Trouble. He appreciated the offer. They were a family and always had each other's backs. "No, I think it's best if we do this alone. We don't know what kinda fucked up mess we're walking into."

"Okay, but one fucking phone call and we're on the next plane, got it?"

"Got it, thanks, man."

"We've got the kids, they can come stay with us in the guest house. Princess will love to have them curl up with her."

"I'll send Herc over to chaperon. He's strangely attached to your weird pets."

"Okay, I'm gonna go get dressed, and we're gonna head out to find Priest a suit. I bet he's sexy as fuck in a suit."

"You're thinking about stripping him out of that suit, ain't ya?"

"You fucking know it," Lucky growled and turned on his toes to head back to Priest. In some fucked up way maybe this was a way for Priest to get closure. To let the past go so Priest could move on. He jogged up the steps and to their room, he paused in the doorway finding Priest's body curled around Plague and Cyclops. Priest's eyes were closed tight as he sobbed quietly.

His heart broke as he rushed to the bed and laid down behind Priest gathering the bigger man in his arms. He pressed tender kisses to Priest's nape, upper back and shoulder, rocking Priest gently as he let Priest grieve. He soaked in Priest's warmth, his clean scent and tried to give him as much of his own strength as he could to the man he'd loved for so long.

10 DESTRUCTION OR REBIRTH

Their flight had been delayed, and they'd barely made it to the cemetery on time. To be honest, Priest wouldn't have minded missing it. The more he thought about it, the less he wanted to see his father or care about what some lawyer had to say the next day.

The bright afternoon sun was cheery considering he stood next to his mother's coffin at the graveside service. They were given a chance to say their goodbyes before she'd be lowered into the ground.

She was exactly how he remembered. Even in death, she retained her ethereal perfection. There was never a hair out of place and her makeup flawless. Priest thought he'd feel something, grief or anger, yet nothing was there. Years of her mental and emotional abuse deadened the love he should have felt for her. She hadn't even questioned the years of missed holidays or phone calls. Did she know what Andre did to him for three years? Would she have even cared? He didn't think so.

He'd exchanged one abusive situation for a worse one. A shiver traveled his spine, and he wrapped his arms around himself to ward off the sudden chill despite the hot day. The familiar and comforting scent of Lucky infused the air around him before lean, muscular arms twined around his waist. He relaxed back into Lucky's strength, and Lucky's chin rested on the top of his head.

He wouldn't have been able to do this without his best friend. Terror stiffened his body at the thought of being without Lucky.

"Shh, you're fine. I can see your mind working overtime with shit you shouldn't be worried about. I ain't going any place."

"Matthew, this is highly inappropriate." His father William Beall's disapproving voice almost made him move away.

"We don't give a fuck what you think is inappropriate. Now you go back to your side, and we'll stay right here until Priest is ready to go."

His lips twitched which really was inappropriate as his father huffed and quietly stormed off.

"What an asshole, are you sure you're not adopted?"

"Lucky," he admonished.

"Fake baby Jesus, I know that tone."

"The Priest is eying you with the intent to probably exorcise us for our evil and homosexual ways."

"Um, have you forgotten we're atheists?"

"No, I haven't forgotten, but at least be respectful, even if their beliefs are insane."

"Fine, I'll just stand here and rub on you until—"

"Luck—"

"Yeah, yeah." Lucky dropped his chin to his shoulder and nuzzled the side of his neck.

He knew what his best friend was doing. Lucky distracted him when things got to be too much. As much as he appreciated it, there was a time and a place, he knew Lucky had no idea about proper time and place. It's one of the things he loved about the man—he never lied or pretended to be something else.

"Don't you have something you want to say to her? Rage, something?"

"She isn't there. It's just a shell and memories."

"Then that's it."

"But shouldn't I feel something?"

"Baby, you feel what you need to feel. You haven't had any contact with her and your dad in four years."

"I want to know why she hated me. Why she couldn't love me or understand."

"Some people just don't have it in them. It's a failing on their part, not yours. You're perfect, and your family is at home waiting for us. Our weird little furry kids."

"I want to go home."

"Then we'll go home, I'll call about changing our flight."

"No, I just have to make it through the reading tomorrow."

"Okay, let's go back to the hotel. Curl up and have some major snuggling. I'll cuddle the fuck out your sexy ass."

He turned in the circle of Lucky's arms and looked up at him. "Appropriate—" A flash of sunlight off metal distracted him, and he turned to look. His lungs froze, and his chest tightened as panic built.

"Priest, what's—"

Andre leaned back against a pristine BMW, he remembered the angelic smile, but he wasn't distracted by it anymore, he knew what was hiding behind it. The sadistic pleasure in inflicting as much pain and humiliation as he could.

"Hey, hey." Strong, calloused hands gripped his face and forced his eyes back to Lucky's. "Breathe, pretty bear."

"It's him."

"Him, the bastard?" The unnatural rage in his sweet pacifist's voice pulled him back.

"Lucky, look at me, please."

"What the fuck is he doing here?"

"Ignore him." It was taking everything inside him to listen to his own advice, but he focused on Lucky. He tugged gently at one of the locs laying against the white, cotton shirt with an intricate embroidered white pattern on either side of the pale wooden buttons. Fingertips dug almost painfully into his hips. "Let's go, you promised me cuddles."

"Yeah, let's go, do you want to say bye to your dad?"

"No, I just want to go." He laced his fingers through Lucky's and pulled him toward where they'd parked the car which unfortunately was in front of Andre's. He tried to swallow around the lump in his throat that was threatening to choke him.

A continuous loop of every punch, slap, and every time Andre used his body no matter how much he protested played inside his head. He tried to stay on his feet as his knees threatened to buckle, but he had to keep Lucky out of jail. Lily would disown him if she had to come to California to bail her son out of jail.

"Hello, Matthew." The sickeningly sweet voice that said he was sorry countless times hit him with the force of a punch.

"What are you doing—" His throat closed up, and he took a deep breath. "Here?"

"I heard your mother passed and wanted to offer my—"

"We don't give a fuck what you wanted, get in your fucking car and go." Lucky's body formed a protective wall between him and Andre.

"Lucky, you said—"

"Priest, get in the car."

"Not without you."

"Got yourself a pretty little guard dog, Matthew? How's your job at Twirled World Ink?"

Andre knew where he worked, probably where he lived. He pressed his forehead to Lucky's back and inhaled, he touched his fingertips to his thumb, counting as he inhaled and exhaled with the rhythm.

"Turned into some biker."

"Lucky, I wanna go home." His voice rasped out as his lungs ached.

"You may like playing your sick little fucking mind game with my man, but I'll tell you right now, you won't fucking win. You get off on inflicting pain, and I can guarantee that shit is over. Priest, baby, get in the car."

Lucky's hand came back and squeezed his thigh, he backed up until he hit the car. He watched as Lucky went toe to toe with the shorter, but much broader Andre. Lucky's fists were clenched at his sides. He didn't like Lucky's anger. It was like the day at the retreat when he'd lied to Lucky, although this was much worse, this spoke of violence. He didn't want to think about Lucky being capable—that's when it happened.

"He needs a heavy hand. Gets mouthy when he's allowed too much freedom—"

Lucky landed an uppercut with his left without Andre having the time to defend himself. Andre stumbled back against his car.

"You're going to fucking pay for that," Andre hissed as he surged toward Lucky.

Lucky's hand landed on Andre's chest and pushed him back against the vehicle.

"I'm already paying for it because the man I love more than anything in this fucking world is scared of me right now. I care more about that than your bullshit threats. Now you're going to leave him the fuck alone or I know several people that'll make your arrogant ass fucking disappear, got me?"

Lucky didn't wait for an answer. He backed up as Lucky approached and put their rental between them.

"Get in the car, baby, we'll go back to the room, and I'll leave you alone for a bit."

He only nodded as he took in the misery in Lucky's gaze. Lucky opened the driver's door and slid into the seat. He got into the passenger side ignoring Andre even thought he could feel the white-hot rage aimed his way. Four years later, he knew the terror of that one look, and it promised punishment. But he wasn't Matthew anymore, he was Priest except he didn't know how to handle Lucky's actions or if he could.

♦ ♦ ♦

The soft tick of a clock sounded almost deafening in the quiet of the room. It had been hours since Lucky had changed quickly and left after dropping him off. It was the longest they'd been apart without a phone call or a text.

They were practically together twenty-four hours a day, and he didn't know if he could handle being without him.

He was still dealing with the aftermath of his panic attack and the knowledge that Lucky defended him. The violence still threw him for a loop. He'd never thought his fun-loving and laid-back Lucky could hit anyone.

His eyes were raw and swollen from crying. It was too much. His mother's death, the unexpected reappearance of Andre and Lucky's actions. All of it combined to warp his image of Lucky mixing it up with Andre. Plus, he felt guilty for those moments he feared Lucky.

He wasn't a stranger to violence in his new life. No one could spend a night at Brawlers without a fight breaking out, but he'd always had Lucky between him and the fight. Lucky was always his protector. The first one to step in to make sure he was happy and safe.

After his mind had cleared and his medicine kicked in, Lucky's words came back to him. Lucky loved him, but it wasn't just friend-type love. The way Lucky treated him, the small things he did without thought. All the nights Lucky opened his bed and arms so that he'd sleep without the nightmares. Lucky looked at him as if he was Lucky's whole world.

He pulled his phone from his sleep pants and his heart stuttered in his chest at the no new messages. He stroked his thumb over the screen and went to tap the shortcut to call Lucky when the click of the lock had him pivoting toward the door.

Lucky's dreads hung around his dropped shoulders. The man's misery was palatable. Lucky closed the door behind him, but stood next to it and shoved his hands into the pockets of his holey jeans. His hand began to ache from where he had it clenched around his phone. Lucky's lashes were damp and spiked, as red as his own.

The silence between them was thick and suffocating.

"Priest, I'm—"

Lucky jerked his hands from his pockets and scrubbed them over his face as he fell back against the wall. A sob caught in Lucky's throat and he curled more into himself.

Priest couldn't take it, he dropped his phone and quickly strode across the room. He wrapped his hands around Lucky's wrists and pulled his hands from his face, tears steadily flowed from Lucky's eyes. Leaning in, he cupped Lucky's face in his hands and placed soft, lingering kisses all over his face, his eyes, cheeks tasting the saltiness wetness. He hesitated when his mouth touched Lucky's and their shuddering breaths mingled.

It was a hesitant dance, advance and retreat in tandem. Their lips barely touching as he darted his gaze repeatedly from Lucky's down to his mouth. It was as if his heart was hammering out of his chest worse than any panic attack he'd ever had. This wasn't the fear, but something else, like the session at the workshop but more intense.

Lucky's lips trembled against his before soft presses, almost as if Lucky was afraid.

"Do you understand how many nights I watched you sleep and wanted to feel you—all of you." Lucky's tentatively traced Priest's lips with the tip of his tongue. "How much I wanted to love you," Lucky asked then slanted his mouth across his.

He felt himself move, Lucky slowly walking him backward toward the bed.

"Why," he asked brokenly.

"I just—"

Lucky laid them on the bed, he realized Lucky turned them onto their sides so he wouldn't feel trapped. The thick ridge of Lucky's dick nudged his own. It was the first time in years he felt a hard cock against his, and he gasped as his body responded.

"Why?"

Lucky's left hand came to rest on his hip and tugged him just a bit closer. He couldn't stop shaking as his body felt as if it were overheating. His face felt on fire. His cock and balls ached, he hadn't felt a physical response in so long. The intensity of it was overwhelming.

"You trusted me. Fuck, I knew bad shit happened before you came to me and you trusted me to hold you…to keep you safe."

Priest worked the buttons on Lucky's shirt free, wanting warm, smooth skin against his hairier body. When his bare chest pressed to the skin he exposed, Lucky shook and groaned arching and rubbing against him.

"S'long, no one since I've had you in my bed."

He froze at Lucky's confession. He'd been sleeping in Lucky's bed off and on since a year after he moved in.

"I don't know if—"

"We're good as is. Just don't leave me, please, Priest."

Another sob shuddered against his mouth. He wrapped his arms around Lucky's neck, and Lucky tucked his head beneath Priest's chin. Tears burned his eyes as Lucky desperately clutched him to his body. They laid there breathing each other in, Priest matched his breaths to Lucky's and felt as they both relaxed. There were so many questions he wanted answers to, but it was already too much for one day. He wanted another night safe in Lucky's arms and to know he never had to be afraid again. Lucky loved him, practically confessed it, but he wasn't as brave, and he hated himself for it.

11 DOES HE KNOW HE'S KILLING ME?

Priest had been right about his mother wanting to humiliate him even after death. He'd sat there holding Priest's hand while he was stripped of any inheritance. His pretty bear didn't give a fuck about things like money or property, but being the subject of condemnation broke another piece of Priest. Priest had been unusually silent since they'd flown home two days before. They'd all tried to get him out of his shell, it was almost like the Priest who had arrived at Twirled four years earlier. Priest hadn't slept in his bed in days, the last night was in the hotel before they'd flown home.

He wasn't the same either. Because of who and what he was he'd been beaten down plenty of times, some of his so-called accidents over the years weren't accidents. He'd learned to fight because he had no other choice, but since Priest came into his life, he hid it never wanting Priest to see him capable. It hadn't worked, the rage had taken over while that bastard said Priest needed a heavy hand.

Priest needed to be loved, treated with gentleness, and he'd done everything in his power to do that for the man he loved. He did love him, not in a friend capacity. He wanted to spend the rest of his life with Priest, wake up with Priest tucked to his side or a Priest blanket with the man fully draped over him. He wanted that inked ring around their fingers. He just wanted the fucking right to tell everyone that Priest was his and not get that look from everyone. The one that said he had no chance.

No one could call him much of a catch. He was skinny and funny looking, he made himself a target just by being him. He did try to be normal once, and it was the worse fucking day of his life. He watched Priest from under his lashes as he pretended to sketch. What if things never went back to the way they were before? What if Priest never wanted to sleep in his bed or touch him just to know he was there?

He didn't think he could survive it. He set this sketchpad aside and stood with his backpack in his hand. "Hey, I'm out, I got somewhere to be," he called out, Priest looked up but didn't offer him that smile that was all Lucky's.

Did Priest realize he was killing him?

He shook his head, he wanted to run from the shop, but he kept his pace slow and lazy. He could feel the looks of pity he'd been getting since he'd told the guys what happened. There was one person who would give him great advice without trying to skewer him with sarcasm or I-told-you-sos. He just hoped he was home.

He hopped on his bike, started it up and sped off in the direction of Scary's house.

＋ ＋ ＋

Twenty minutes later, he stood on Scary's porch and knocked on the door, Elijah's car was parked in the driveway. Tank's bike wasn't there, and he knew Scary was at the shop until dinner time with Elijah, Sophie and Tank then off to Brawlers. Soft footsteps sounded on the other side, and the door opened to reveal a surprised Elijah.

"I fucked up."

"That's nothing new, but come on in. Coffee?" Elijah reached out and grabbed his forearm pulling him into the house. Sophie would be at school for another two hours.

"No, I'm okay."

"Okay, come on in the office, I have to send an email, and then I'm done for the day."

"If you're busy I can—"

"Shut up and get in my office."

"Being with Scary and Tank has fucking corrupted you, and I mean that literally."

"None of your bullshit—"

"Cussing, pod person Elijah."

"Yeah, yeah, they've ruined me. So start talking."

"You know we went to Priest's mother's funeral."

"I heard that was a clusterfuck. Scary's words, not mine."

Elijah walked toward what he knew Scary had turned into an office for Elijah to work from home. Elijah walked behind the desk and set down.

"Yeah, that's a fucking understatement. I don't want to give away Priest's secrets."

"Anyone who knows Priest can tell that's he's had a bad time of it, and I don't need details, that's something between you and him. So just give it to me from your side."

"First Priest's mom dies, his dad has a lawyer call to inform him and tell him about the reading. That turned into everyone around Priest getting some bullshit inheritance while he sat there getting stared at and treated like a fucking leper."

"That had to be hard for him. To leave that and have it thrown into his face on the day he can't get closure because his mom isn't around the tell him why."

"She blamed him for what happened to him, fucking blamed him. Like he asked for that fucker—" He cut it off, he didn't want to give away secrets not his to give, but it was going to be tough as fuck to tell Elijah only half the story and get the advice he needed.

Elijah finished sending whatever he had to and after he stood, coming to sit on the couch beside him. He curled his legs under him. "Parents aren't always fit for the job. Our parents weren't, and I turned into a twelve-year-old taking care of an infant while they were off still partying and traveling. But I'm sure what we went through is nowhere near what he did."

"I punched someone—"

"You? Pacifist, hippie Lucky Trenton resorted to violence."

"Yeah, yeah, me, but you've seen me—"

"I know, you've gotten into a few fights at Brawlers but you were always between Priest and danger, so it isn't the first time."

"I threw the first punch. Fuck!" He dropped his face into his hands and scrubbed them over his stinging eyes. He wouldn't fucking cry again. "When I saw his face, I knew I fucked up. He was frightened of me—me. I've loved him from almost the minute I saw him. He was so big and sweet, shy, that little belly of his—"

Elijah chuckled and ran his fingers through his thick curls before resting his head in his hand. "No one that sees you around him thinks your feelings are anything platonic."

"Priest does."

"When you're in an abusive relationship, and you get out, every experience is colored by it. The way you see yourself and the world around you, people that treat you kindly have ulterior motives. I'm not saying it's always the case, but depending on the severity, it takes years to work through it, and sometimes people never do."

"We kissed."

"You always kiss, people that don't know y'all already think you're a couple."

"No, the night before we left, a real kiss, but he told me he didn't think he'd ever be ready. I told him we were fine as is."

"You lied to him." The shock in Elijah's voice was clear.

"I did because I don't want him to leave me. I'll take the nights of cuddling him or the touches that won't ever lead anywhere, I can live with that if I have him."

"You're setting yourself up as a martyr, Lucky. How long has it been since you've been with someone other than Priest?"

"Three years, since the first night he spent in my bed. I knew I could never have him, so I tried to forget how I felt in hook ups, but it never worked, and I always felt guilty when I'd see him the day after like I fucking cheated."

"Does he know that?"

"I told him it's been no one but him since we started sleeping together."

"Listen, this is my advice, it's nothing but an opinion, but Priest needs space. His past in all it's fucked-uppedness was thrown in his face. All that brutality and pain, the emotional damage is back, and it's like reprocessing it all over again. It's like going back to step one and seeing you resort to violence, his vision of you has been colored by your actions and his past. All mixed up and warped."

"But what the fucker said, Priest is the sweetest and loving man I ever met. He's perfect and someone being able to say those things—to suggest Priest needs a heavy hand. How could anyone put their hands on Priest without any other intent besides loving him?"

"People are fucked up in the head, you know how hard it was for Juvie to adjust from what she went through to living with us. She's still not exactly settled, sometimes she still has moments when she feels unsafe. We talk her through it and make sure she knows that she's loved and permanent in our lives. That her Daddy, Dad and Papa love her more than anything. You just need to reestablish what you and Priest had. No, it won't ever be the same, but maybe, in the end, this will strengthen what you two have."

"I don't ever see that happening, you didn't see his face."

"Then give him some space, some time to think and analyze what happened. The kiss has to mean something, it's s small step, but maybe a move forward. I have to go get Juvie and Princess from school in about forty-five minutes, you want to hang out?"

"No, I think I need a bit of a ride to clear my head. It's been awhile."

"Then…" Elijah cupped his face and leaned forward to kiss his brow.

"What the fuck, this better—" Scary roared from the doorway and Elijah laughed.

"Oh, please, like I can handle another man, you and Tank are more than I can deal with now." Elijah slid off the couch and went to Scary and lifted onto his toes to kiss the man's frown. "Lucky, take your ride, get your fucking head straight and have a long heart-to-heart with Priest. Don't let it fester."

"Thanks, Elijah."

"You coming with to get our daughter and niece or are you going to brood?"

"I was hoping for a quickie."

"I've got thirty, you up to the challenge?" Elijah's voice was flirty.

"Bedroom," Scary ordered.

"And I'm gone, that's just fucking disturbing."

Lucky escaped as quickly as possible and found himself a half hour outside of town with no idea how he got there. The road was deserted, the sun was shining and the rumble of the engine loud in his ears. He couldn't remember the last time he'd been out on his own.

He tapped his toe to change gear and took off faster, safe in the knowledge no cops were around to ticket him. He savored the wind in his face and the scent of hot tar baking under the sun. For a few hours, he wanted to lose himself. Find his center, he needed Priest, he just had to figure out how to get his man back.

A horn sounded behind him seconds before his bike was bumped, his back end spun out, and nothing would save him from the long skid and possible road rash. His bike went sideways, the pain excruciating, but the bumper rammed into his helmet sending him into a spin off the side of the road. All he knew was pain as he felt himself flying off the side the embankment, the smell of smoke hit him just as everything went black.

12 WHERE THE FUCK IS LUCKY?

The asshole in the police uniform in front of him was quickly pissing him off. "He always comes home."

"Mr. Beall, I'm sorry, but as Mr. Trenton is an adult and there's nothing to prove he isn't just spending the night away from the house."

"Listen, he always comes home, and he never goes this long without calling me. I want to file a missing—"

"He's been supposedly missing for eight hours, I'm sorry, but department policy is we can't look into a report until at least forty-eight hours has passed unless you have some reason or proof to prove foul play."

"I know Lucky, and he wouldn't worry me—"

"I'm sorry about your—partner."

He hated that damn pause. Homophobic asshole.

"I don't give a shit about forty-eight hours, my Lucky wouldn't do this to me."

"I'm sorry, but you'll have to come back in two days."

"Fine, if you won't do shit but sit on your fat, donut-eating ass…" Priest spun on his toes and headed for the door. "I'll take care of it myself."

He pulled out his phone and called Lily.

"Priest, is my least fucked up child showing his ass again?" Lily's voice was filled with amusement, and that didn't bode well.

"So, Lucky isn't there?"

"What do you mean is he here?"

"He hasn't come home. Lucky never—"

"Did you go to the police station?"

"Yes, but they're saying they can't do anything until he's missing for forty-eight hours."

"Why didn't you fucking call before now?"

"I didn't want to worry you until—"

"That's no excuse. Get everyone to Twirled House, Damon and I will be there soon."

She'd disconnected the call before he had a chance to answer. He stood beside his bike and stared down at his phone. He'd already told Zerk and Landon, Trouble and Brody. He hit the speed dial for Elijah.

"Priest?" A sleepy Elijah answered the phone.

"Lucky's missing."

"What…when? I just saw him this afternoon."

"He came to see you, when?"

"It was about one, we talked for about an hour, and then he took off saying he needed to go for a ride."

"Where was he going?"

"I'm sorry, he didn't say."

"Oh, was he okay when he left."

There was a long pause on the other end. "He was a little upset. He needed someone to talk to. Let me call Scary and Tank, is everyone meeting up at the house?"

104

"Yes, Lily and Damon are on their way. I'm leaving the police station, they won't let me file a report until he's been missing—"

"Forty-eight hours. He's an adult."

"I don't care if he's an adult. He wouldn't stay out this late without at least texting me."

"We'll take care of it, Priest, get home, and we'll figure it all out."

"What did he have to talk to you—"

"I don't feel comfortable saying. He needed to talk."

"About me," he asked.

"I'll see you in a few, Priest."

He disconnected the call and shoved his phone into the pocket of his jacket. He lifted his hands and covered his face as another round of tears began, but he didn't have time. What if he was just out for a ride?

Nothing had been right between them since the funeral. It had taken everything in him not to go to Lucky's bed. To just curl up beside him and be okay again. He threw his leg over the seat of his bike, he started it quickly and headed toward home.

♦ ♦ ♦

The sun was just cresting the horizon, and they'd transitioned from copious amounts of coffee to Zerk's supply of energy drinks. He was sitting on the couch with Cyclops curled on his lap and Plague on his shoulder. He absently stroked Cyclops folded ears.

"Let's go over the time line again." Scary leaned forward and rested his forearms on his knees.

"He left the shop about twelve-thirty," Priest answered.

"Lucky got to our place at one."

"What were you two talking about?" That was Lily.

"Things were tense between Priest and him. He was a bit down, and I think he wanted some advice that wasn't littered with sarcasm and get all y'all telling him I told you so." Elijah glared at everyone from his spot tucked under Tank's arm in front of the fireplace.

"We're not that much a group of dicks."

"Yes, you all are. I told him to go have a heart to heart with Priest and not let it all fester, but he said he was going for a ride to clear his head. After that, he left."

"Well, now that it's daylight, we'll all gear up and head out in different directions maybe he broke down. Anyone tried to call him recently." Scary stood and lifted his arms over his head in a long stretch.

Tank kissed Elijah, then stood and headed for the door.

"I'll just put Plague in her cage and be back." He set Cyclops on the floor then got to his feet and headed upstairs to Lucky's bedroom. The room that use to be theirs. He eased Plague into her cage and secured the latch. He turned to the made bed, but he could still see the impression of Lucky's long frame on his side.

Wrapping his arms around his stomach, he let his chin fall to his chest as he started to cry. The tears hot against his cheeks. He hadn't fully realized how much Lucky was a part of his life. All those touches and stupid jokes just to make him smile, it started the moment they'd met. These last two nights he'd snuggled in a lonely bed unable to get warm. He didn't care if Lucky hated him for pulling away or decided he was too much trouble, he just wanted Lucky back.

"Priest." Lily's voice came from so close beside him, and he opened his eyes.

"I want him back."

"We all do, but we have to find him first. You know how accident prone he is. He's going to have some crazy fucking story about having to camp out and eat bark to stay alive."

"I fucked up. He hit my ex while we—"

"He told me. My son tells me everything. You were frightened of him for what he did. He understands that, and he should have thought ahead, measured the consequences, but when someone threatened you—the man he loves, he just lost it for a minute. My son would never, I mean never do anything to purposely hurt you. But when you pulled away you took away his center. You've grounded him so much."

"We need to get going, he missed dinner, and it got pretty cold last night. He hates being cold."

Lily kissed his cheek and smiled at him, and he tried to ignore the pity in her eyes that were exactly like Lucky's.

It didn't take them long to head off in different directions. He'd chosen the route they'd taken on their last solo ride. There was a diner in the middle of nowhere that sold these twenty-pound burgers that if someone finished one they got their picture on some wall of fame. Lucky joked he was going to do it one day. Trouble rode to his left and slightly behind.

If, no when he got Lucky back he would make it up to Lucky for being an asshole. He'd sleep beside Lucky every night. Tell him he loved him. Everything he'd been frightened to say he'd get out no matter how painful. He missed the scent of lemon and hemp lotion, he missed the softness of Lucky's locs across his chest and stomach. Only eighteen hours and it was as if his heart was being ripped out, they'd never been away from each other more than an hour or two in four years.

He scanned the road ahead, they'd been going for almost an hour and still nothing. They were about to pass a farm on the right when he noticed a break in the fence with skid marks leading toward it. He motioned toward the side of the road, and he caught Trouble's nod. He slowed and pulled to the side, the acrid scent of smoke made him crinkle his nose.

Curiosity turned to terror as he noticed a phone smashed on the side of the road. He knocked his kickstand down with his heel, he tore off his helmet as he took off running. His legs buckled at the sight of Lucky lying pinned beneath the remains of his bike. He slid down the embankment screaming Lucky's name.

Falling to his knees beside Lucky, he reached out but hesitated not knowing where to touch. There was a crack along the right side of his helmet, blood coated what skin wasn't bruised, lacerated or bore road rash.

"Trouble," he hollered.

"I'm calling, is he—"

"I don't know," he choked out as he bent forward. "Lucky, can you—"

He didn't dare move him, but he laid his head on Lucky's chest, listening for the familiar and comforting rhythm of his heart. His breath shuddered in short-lived relief, it was the strong, steady beat that lulled him to sleep at night. Then he noticed the soft panting breaths as if he couldn't breathe deep enough.

"State police are on their way and a chopper, we're too far out for an ambulance to do—"

He blocked it out, he didn't want to hear any more. He moved his gaze over Lucky cataloging each injury. Lucky's body was posed at weird angles, the denim of his left leg was blackened and burned. There was so much blood—too much. He gently took Lucky's hand, making sure not to move it, but needing to touch him, even in a small way. Lucky was so cold. Priest jerked off his jacket and laid it over Lucky.

"You're gonna be so cranky when you wake up. I'll make sure you get a lot of warm blankets, but you—you gotta wake up for me. I'm so sorry, baby, I didn't—I didn't mean it. I was just stupid. I'll make it better I promise."

As he spoke, tears flowed down his cool cheeks as he softly stroked Lucky's hand, traced the lines of Lucky's bloody palm. He didn't know how much time passed, but suddenly sirens and the loud beat of propellers broke through the eerie quiet.

"Sir, we need to check him, sir," A firm, but gentle voice urged him to step back, and hands were on his shoulders, pulling at him and panic stole through him.

"Dude, no, I got him, don't touch." Trouble started whispering soothing words in his ear as the taller man slowly moved him back away from Lucky. "Breath, Priest, it'll be fine. Let them do their jobs."

"What's his name?" A paramedic in a blue flight suit asked as they began to assess his injuries.

"Lee Trenton."

"White male, single person motorcycle accident. He appears to be in his late twenties multiple blunt trauma to the sternum, possible broken ribs, leg and arm. Pulse weak. Hypothermia and blood loss. Definite head trauma. We need a backboard now."

"I've lost the pulse."

It was the last thing he heard before his legs went out from under him and everything seemed to move in slow motion.

"Priest, pull it together, man, we've gotta get to the hospital."

"You've gotta call—"

"I called everyone, we gotta go."

"I can't lose him, Trouble, I didn't get to tell him—"

"He's gonna be fine, you can get all sappy when he wakes up and when he's back on his feet you can bitch him out."

He watched helplessly as Lucky was loaded into the chopper and it quickly took off. The troopers wanted to ask questions, he answered automatically so he could get going. He didn't realize how slow time could pass until he had to make the long ride to Atlanta.

13 IMMEDIATE FAMILY ONLY

The strong scents of antiseptic stung his nose, and the florescent lights were killing his eyes. He glared at the woman through the partition who was barring him from getting to Lucky. "What do you mean I can't know his condition," Priest yelled at the admitting nurse.

"I'm sorry only immediate family—"

"He's my partner, I have every right—"

"I'm sorry, sir, but hospital policy is very clear, are you married?"

"No." Priest's shoulders slumped, and everything seemed to collapse around him. Lily and Damon were still a half an hour away.

"Mr. Beall, I am extremely sorry, if I could give you the information you wanted, I would."

He could sense the sincerity in her voice and the way she looked at him. "But his parents are still almost half hour away."

"If anything happens and his condition worsens before they get here, I will let you know. It's the best—"

"I understand."

"Here." Trouble thrust a paper cup into his hand and steered him toward a row of uncomfortable looking chairs.

"They won't tell me anything, he's mine I should—"

"Lily and Damon will be here soon. Drink, you need the caffeine, you look like you're about to lose your shit."

"About to? I lost it the moment I saw, I saw him. I can't lose him, he can't leave me."

"He won't, Lucky is a stubborn fuck, and the one thing he cares about above all else is how his pretty bear is."

"What if he's already gone and they just won't tell me."

"Quit," Trouble ordered.

"Who has the kids?"

"Brody stayed behind, he's going to send them to school, and once we know more, we'll tell them what happened. If need be, he'll bring them here."

"You mean to say—"

"Don't piss me off right now, Priest."

He let the conversation go and leaned back, his legs bounced as he kept his eyes fixed on automatic doors.

A short time later Lily and Damon rushed through the entrance, her red-rimmed eyes frantically searched for him and then she was there with her arms wrapped around him.

"What have they said?"

"They won't tell me, I'm not family—"

"The fuck you're not, come with me." Lily had an envelope clutched tightly to her chest.

"My name is Lily Trenton, I'm Lee Trenton's mother, this is my son's partner."

"I've explained—"

"I don't give a fuck what you explained, this is something you'll understand." Lily slammed the Manila envelope onto the desk. "Those are medical power of attorney forms giving Matthew Beall complete control of all medical decisions. Now tell him what the fuck he wants to know."

"Mr. Trenton is in critical condition. He's being prepped for emergency surgery to repair ribs that punctured a lung and also other multiple fractures. They'll know more when they open him up."

"Can we see him before they take him?"

"Follow me, I can give you ten minutes."

"Thank you." He took Lily's hand, and they followed the nurse. She moved quickly on sensible shoes through the automatic doors.

"Ten minutes."

He nodded but hesitated to push aside the curtain.

"It's okay, I'm right here." Lily held tight to his hand as she stood close beside him.

He reached out and pushed the curtain aside, his lungs froze in his chest at the sight in front of him. The hiss of the ventilator and the beep of the heart monitor was nothing in comparison to the still bloody and broken body of Lucky.

"We've put him into a medically induced coma. Once he's out of surgery, we'll remove the vent." A soft hand came to rest on his forearm and a compassionate, slightly rounded faced nurse smiled up at him. "It looks scary, but it's necessary."

"You removed his piercings."

"Yes, we're going to do an MRI to check for any damage we can't visually assess."

"Did you remove his Guiche?"

"Guiche?"

"It's a piercing through the perineum."

"Oh no, we didn't even think..." the nurses face turned red. "We did remove his—"

"Prince Albert."

"I'll let someone know about the other so it can be removed before his scan. I'll leave you alone with your husband. Here." she placed a small braided band of silver in his palm.

It was Lucky's favorite ring, he'd worn it on his ring finger for—three years. He closed his hand around the body warmed silver. "He's not—" How he wished he could say yes, claim Lucky for all to see, but he'd waited too long.

"Thank you." Lily cut him off and nudged him toward the bed.

"Riding for him is like second nature. His bike's always been like an extension of him."

"We don't know what happened out on that road. An animal could've darted in front of him. Any number of things." Lily placed herself on the other side of the bed. "He was always my daredevil. There wasn't anything he wouldn't try." She reached out and stroked her hand over Lucky's locs.

"Fearless, I love that about him. I love him you know, always have." It was always more than friends. He pushed it away, denied the truth that Lucky so treasured and now he was possibly going to lose him. Before he could say it aloud, or a real a kiss, one not platonic or their one kiss caused by stress and desperation—a moment to just know they were what each other wanted. And what had he'd done? He pushed Lucky away, denied himself and Lucky the comfort of sleeping in each other's arms. The last memory of him would be his indifference. He hadn't even said goodbye.

"I know. Lucky's blind as fuck, but none of the rest of us were."

"I treated him so—"

"A man who brutalized you and invited others to do the same, my son defended you. No matter what he says, he didn't regret it. The only thing he regretted was the way he caused you to look at him. I knew my son loved you the moment he brought you to dinner that first time."

"How?"

"He treated you like Damon does me. Damon gets some intense satisfaction from knowing I'm cared for, and Lucky does the same for you. Do you know he bought a house?"

"No, when?"

"A year ago, I shouldn't have told you, it was going to be a surprise. He said it was your perfect house, the one you dreamed of having."

"I told him that years ago." He wanted a small cottage on a few acres, a home like Lily's with character and infused with love and laughter.

"You made my son happy. Made him believe that he could have someone all his own even as goofy and crazy as he is." Lily leaned down and rested her lips on Lucky's forehead ignoring the blood, dirt and bandages.

He listened to her softly whisper she loved him.

"He's perfect."

Lily straightened with tears in her eyes. "I'm not one to lie, honesty—" She stroked Lucky's brow. "We're not given very many chances in this world for happiness. It's a shit place to live, but you were given a chance to be loved and cherished. Don't fuck it up and if he doesn't make it, a treasure that you were loved above even himself. You were his enlightenment and his joy—his soul mate."

Priest nodded and watched her walk away before he leaned down to place his mouth next to Lucky's ear. "You have to come back to me, you have to show me our house—" His voice broke. "I need you. I need you to love me until I know that I never have to be afraid again."

"I'm sorry, but we need to get him upstairs."

"Okay." He wiped at his eyes and then pressed his lips to Lucky's brow. "I love you." He straightened and stepped back as they started to wheel him out.

He didn't want to think it was the end. Didn't want to believe that this would be the last time he saw Lucky with his heart beating. He wanted to see Lucky's beautiful eyes open, staring into his while he told Lucky he loved him. Sorrow broke him at all the years he'd wasted living in the past, believing touch only led to pain. Denying what he'd always sensed to be true—Lucky was his.

14 LUCKY'S NOT WAKING UP

Lucky's chest rose and fell in deep even rhythm, Priest carefully curled up on Lucky's right side. Three days passed since he'd found Lucky and still Lucky hadn't awakened. He talked to him for hours. They said Lucky may be able to hear him, but part of him hoped not. He'd rambled on about plans for them, when they'd move into their house, and how much he missed sleeping in their bed.

Everyone tried to talk him into going home to get some sleep. He'd refused, he couldn't sleep without Lucky, not since the first night three years ago when Lucky found him pacing the halls. Lucky offered him a spot beside him, and he hadn't been able to drift off without the warmth of Lucky's body beside him. He still didn't understand what made him agree as quickly as he had.

He rested his head on Lucky's uninjured shoulder and tenderly stroked Lucky's hairless chest. Lucky lost too much blood before they'd found him. They'd repaired his lung with surgery and thankfully hadn't found anything serious during the operation. The swelling of his brain had subsided, but he just wasn't waking up. The doctors and nurses kept telling him the same thing, Lucky would wake up when his body was ready.

"Good evening, Priest, how's he doing?" Meg, a pretty middle-aged nurse, breezed in with a bright smile with a clipboard in her hands.

Meg didn't even bat an eye seeing him on the bed with Lucky. One of the other nurses had tried to tell him he couldn't sleep there. No one else said a word. Meg came over to the bed and checked the machines and recorded everything on Lucky's chart.

"Still not awake."

"I know, but they just stopped the meds last night. He's doing great, his vitals are strong, and his color is looking better. He'll be awake before you know it."

"I hope so, it's weird not hearing him talk. He loves to talk about anything and everything. I always said I hated it, but I really want him to wake up so I can hear him call me his pretty bear."

"I've been catching bits and pieces of stories about you two. He appears to love you very much."

"I love him too, I want him to wake up so I can tell him."

He reached up and stroked Lucky's beard, after days of no trimming Lucky was looking a bit scraggly.

"Like I said, he'll be awake soon and you two can make up for lost time."

"Thank you."

Her smile became even brighter. "I'll be back to check on you two later. His doctor is going to peek in soon."

"Okay."

"Now, try to get some rest, he's looking better than you." She patted his hand where it rested it over Lucky's heart, then disappeared.

The opening of the door had him looking up again to find Linus walking in with a large cloth bag in his left hand.

"Hey, I thought Lou was coming tonight."

"She got stuck at work, some emergency meeting or whatever. I took off early to bring you a few changes of clothes and Lucky some sleep pants. No one needs to see his fuzzy ass when he's up and moving around." Linus set the bag on the chair next to the bed and opened it. "There were some books beside the bed, but I didn't know whose side was whose, so I just grabbed both stacks and the tablet, plus charger. Trouble sent replacement jewelry for what they cut out and new plugs for what got misplaced."

"Thanks, Lucky will feel more like himself with his stuff back in. Did you bring his shampoo and dread oil, also his hair dryer?"

"Yeah, Lou texted me what I needed to grab. He has more hair product than Lou."

"Dreads take a bit of upkeep."

"Well, everything's in the bag. Do you want to shower while I'm here," Linus asked as he lifted the bag off the chair and sat down.

"Yeah, are your parents on their way?"

"They were napping when I left, but I'm sure they'll be headed this way soon. The crew said they'd come in shifts tomorrow."

"They were here all day yesterday."

"How are you holding up?"

"I'm worried and exhausted, I really want us to be in our bed. This bed doesn't exactly accommodate both of us, but—"

"You're not going to sleep anywhere else."

Priest nodded, he inhaled the scent of hemp lotion he'd applied after Lucky's sponge bath earlier.

"Thank you for—"

"Don't mention it. Now, go shower, I can smell you from here."

"I took a shower yesterday." He eased off the bed, then leaned down to press his mouth to Lucky's dry lips. "There's swabs on the table."

"I got it, Priest, go relax for a few minutes."

He kissed Lucky once more. He straightened and walked around the bed to grab the bag Linus brought. Picking it up he headed for the bathroom, stepped inside, and closed the door behind him. He set the bag on the shower chair. With quick movements, he untied his boots, removed them and his socks, and then removed the rest of his clothes. He shivered at the chill in the air. Why the hell did they keep hospitals so damn cold?

He reached into the stall and turned the taps, checking the temperature to make sure it was hot enough. He stepped beneath the spray. The scalding hot water hit him on his nape and cascaded down his back. Laying his hands flat against the wall he leaned forward to press his forehead to the cool tile. He let the tears flow. That was the only place he allowed himself to break down. Losing Lucky wasn't an option. He couldn't be afraid anymore, and he needed a future with Lucky. He hated himself for being pessimistic.

Growing angry with himself, he pushed away from the wall and washed his hair in quick, rough strokes. His emotions were too raw. Even with Lucky close by, their fingers linked as he attempted to sleep, the nightmares pushed at his mind. The hands holding him down. The laughter and grunts as his body was forced to submit. In his dream he repeatedly screamed, begged for them to stop—for Andre to stop them.

"Priest," Linus called his name through the door jerked him from the memories.

As he slowly came back to reality, he heard his own loud agonized sobs echoing off the tiled walls. The water had grown cold. He quickly got out, dried off and dressed. He scrubbed roughly at his face knowing his eyes were red and puffy. He'd taken long, cleansing breaths before he opened the door.

Linus stood there with a frown on his face—a face too similar to Lucky's. Linus opened his arms.

Linus must have noticed his hesitation because he smiled sadly.

"Come on, Priest, I know I'm not as homely as you like and I'm a bit out of practice, but I've been told I give good hugs."

He stepped into the opened arms, they weren't Lucky's and the body wasn't lean, didn't smell of lemon and hemp, but it was okay. This wasn't the past.

"You'll be okay," Linus whispered and stroked his hair. "He'll wake up and be as annoying as fuck."

He tightened his arms around Linus' bulky frame.

"I knew you were gay. Now you're making moves on my man," Lucky's broken and slightly pissed off voice came from the bed.

"Did you hear that? The evil one has awoken." Linus held on.

"Hey, mine," Lucky growled, and it was kind of cute.

He pulled away from Linus and was across the room in seconds, he leaned over the bed to hold Lucky's face.

"Don't you ever do this to me again," he ordered and before Lucky could answer, Priest kissed him. Not the friendly teasing ones from the past, but like the hotel, all desperation and long held need. He broke the kiss and looked down into Lucky's tired, glassy eyes.

"Hospitals make you kiss me, I'll remember—"

"I will kill you if you do this again." He closed his eyes. "I'm sorry, this is—"

"No, don't say it. It wasn't your fault. I ruined—"

"You didn't ruin anything," Priest assured and pushed the call button.

Meg walked in, then the chaos began. The questions and tests, he was pushed to the side as they took care of Lucky, but not for a moment did Lucky stop looking at him. Why didn't he ever notice before? So much existed in that expressive gaze that he had overlooked living in the past. The past was gone even though the ripples still affected his present, but they weren't as oppressive as before. He had so much to make up for, and he wasn't going to waste it.

"Pretty bear," Lucky called him.

A smile tilted his lips, and he put away the thoughts, for now, later he'd decide how to put his plans for their future into action. Right then, he needed to reassure himself it wasn't a dream and Lucky was really awake— back with him.

15 HE'S NOT THAT MUCH OF A KLUTZ

Everything he had hurt, there wasn't a part of him that didn't scream in agony every time he moved, but he hid it for Priest. His pretty bear had sunken eyes and dark half-moons under them. Priest's freckles stood out even darker against his pale face. He just kept searching his brain to remember what happened.

Yes, he was accident prone as fuck, but being on his bike was like having an extension of himself. Riding was natural and in thirteen years since he'd first learned to ride, he'd never once had an accident. Although the more he pushed, the darker and painful it became. He'd finally broken his already fucked up brain permanently.

"You're frowning and scrunching up your forehead. Don't think so hard. You know you don't have that many brain cells left."

"Don't be mean, I'm wounded and without jewelry. I can't believe you let those fuckers cut them out."

"Hey, it wasn't like I had much of a choice, they'd already done it before your mother showed up with those papers you never told me about."

Fuck, he hadn't even thought about the papers. He done it when he'd bought the house he'd never told Priest about. If something happened to him, he wanted his—Priest to have his dream cottage. He'd even had his parents do up the outside like theirs because Priest almost seemed to love it. He'd even gone crazy with wind chimes. He bought different ones from all over the world.

The sound of metal tinkling drew his attention.

"Is that—"

"A present from Trouble."

"Gimme, gimme, gimme!" He made a grabby hand with his right hand that wasn't encased in plaster.

"Are you going to put them in yourself?"

"Dammit, don't tease me, I feel so—naked."

Priest stood, set on the bed and nudged his hip. With efficient movements Priest put in a pair of dark wood plugs, then the rest of his piercings including the nipple ones. Even in extreme pain, the intensity of Priest's touch cause his dick to jump, but at least he didn't tent the thin gown and blanket he wore. Two pieces of steel remained, and he knew they weren't going in today, at least not until he could get Trouble to do it. His Guiche and Prince Albert would have to wait.

"Trouble can do the other two." The thought of Trouble touching him even for something as innocent as reinserting his piercings was distasteful.

"I'll just put these in your bag."

"Where is everyone?"

"Catching up on sleep and everything else."

"Maybe you should go home and get some sleep, check on our kids."

"I'm waiting on the next shift to show up. We're running out of clothes, laundries piling up and your temporary bed isn't exactly comfortable for two."

"Are we ever going to be us again?" He hated the distance. Right then, all he wanted was to reach out and pull Priest into his arms like he would've done before. It killed him he felt he didn't have the right. He'd lost count over the years of the times Priest slept beside him. How many times he'd held him or simply touched Priest to calm himself, he'd done it every day for three years.

"Why did you hit him?"

Priest's voice was so small, and it reminded him of that first year after coming to Twirled.

"I've fought and protected you before, why does this time have to be different?"

"Because this is the first time some guy didn't throw the first punch, so answer me, why?"

"Because of every time I've watched you cry in your fucking sleep when you wouldn't come to my bed. For every time you flinched when I reached for you. For every time I've wanted to tell you I love you. Do you know what it felt like when that fucker looked me in the eyes and told me you needed to be hit? All I remembered is what he did to you. I need you to live without fear and to be happy. I don't care if you will ever love me like I do you, but I—"

Priest's soft lips and thick beard tickled his mouth, and he tasted the salt of Priest's tears. He closed his eyes at the ultra-light touch and sensed Priest's hesitation.

"You don't—" His words ceased as Priest's kissed him. A real fucking kiss. Priest's arms twined around his neck, and he placed his hands on Priest's little love handles. He tried to push upward and pain sliced through his side.

"Oh shit, fuck!" He dropped his head back as he breathed through the fire coursing through his ribs.

"I'm so sorry, sorry, let me call the nurse."

"No, no, I'm fine." He so wasn't, but no way was he telling Priest that. "It's okay, just give me a minute and we can try—"

"No repeats, not until you're healed. I do love you, but I'm terrified."

"Of me?"

"Me, how can I have a normal relationship with what happened? How can I ever—"

He lifted his hand and placed it on Priest's cheek, rubbing his thumb over his furry skin. Priest tilted his head pushing into his touch. He urged Priest forward and brought their mouths together, he traced the masculine lines of Priest's lips. He nipped the lower lip and sucked on it gently.

"Who the fuck defines what's normal? We've practically been dating for years and don't even bring sex into it. I know what you're thinking, and fucking stop it."

"But you're a sexual person, won't you—"

"I said stop it. Sex isn't all about penetration. It's about touch and intimacy, just being together."

"Like at that workshop?"

He nodded his head rubbing their mouths together. It seemed like a lifetime since he'd touched and kissed Priest. He'd lived for these moments, but it was so much more significant—like a promise.

"Aw, ain't you two just cute as fuck." Lou's singsong voice came from way too close.

He turned his head to find her mere inches from their faces. "I could've absorbed you in the womb as I am the superior twin."

"Wow, fetus cannibalism, you're a fucking sicko." Lou grinned from ear to ear.

"How did you not kill each other from zygote stage?"

He heard the laughter in Priest's voice and glanced at him to see the beautiful smile curving his man's lips. It was carefree and open, fuck, he wanted to see more of that. He turned back to Lou to glare at her as she just smiled like a mental patient.

"I showed great restraint."

"I kicked him in the nuts all the time, that's why he only has one."

"Hey, I have two beautiful nuts, big and hairy, more than a handful. Perfect for rolling like Chinese Meditation Balls."

"Do they chime like Baoding balls too? I know how you like your jewelry, maybe you have some bells attached to these epic balls of divine design."

"Kiss my hairy ass, you just have ball envy, you wished you had a pair of your own."

"I do see." Lou cupped her breasts. "And mine are bigger, and I can show them off in public in skimpy shirts, while you would go to jail for indecent exposure as is fitting for a pervert such as yourself."

"I'm going, you two can finish this one without me."

Priest looked trapped between horror and amusement.

"No, wait, I wasn't done with you."

"You need siblings bonding time, and as you're both in a hospital, any injuries from you attempting to kill each other can be mended."

Priest kissed him again but avoided his arms when he tried to grab him. Which was probably for the best because his ribs were still fucked.

"You two behave, next shift is here in two hours, I'll try to make sure it's not another Trenton."

He watched Priest walk away.

"You're totally checking out the bear's ass and a fine one it is."

"He's gay."

"I've never poached a day in my life, not one of your men anyway. Although I did get one of Linus' girlfriends alone that one Christmas." Lou waggled her brows.

"Oh, I thought we promised to never speak of that one. Mama nearly lost her buzz when she walked in on that, I know I did."

"Yeah, that one was a mistake of the highest order, but I was high and horny."

"And let's change the subject."

"Okay, how could you be such a fucking moron? Crashing your bike in the middle of nowhere."

"I don't know. I've never once fucked up on my bike—never."

"Well, what the fuck happened then?"

"Can't remember a damn thing. They said it's normal with the head trauma and it probably won't ever come back. It's driving me crazy. I'm not that much of a klutz."

"Well, everyone is pissed and want answers, so you better get to thinking." She walked around to the opposite side of the bed and laid down beside him. "And don't do that to me again."

"Promise."

"Any hot nurses or doctors around here? Always wanted to get nasty with sexiness in scrubs."

"I thought you did that on your last seventy-two-hour hold?"

"Didn't count, I was medicated to the max and thought the orderly was a nurse. Total fucking letdown."

"There's this pretty nurse, completely your type, appears to be the three F's."

"Oh, man, you know how I love them fluffy, freaky and flexible."

The conversation devolved from there as he reconnected with his twin who he didn't spend enough time with lately. He had a lot of shit to think about. Priest's kiss, the I love you, and how the fuck he ended over an embankment in the middle of nowhere. First, he had to get home, back to his bed, his man and their kids.

16 HE SHOULDN'T BE HERE

He hated grocery shopping, but luckily, they only needed a few things. If it wasn't for him, the guys would starve.

"Priest," Brody called his name from his spot at one of the four registers.

He walked toward Brody who was wiping down the belt. "Did the guys shop for anything other than coffee and energy drinks while I was with Lucky?"

"Nope." Brody popped the P in Princess fashion. "But they've been doing a lot of takeout unless Zerk cooks. No one else wants to brave food poisoning."

"Women would be so much—"

"No, they won't, same problems just different causes."

"Celibacy is the way to go."

Brody laughed so hard he snorted. "I like my Trouble time a little too much for that."

"Don't remind me, I was so glad when we moved y'all to the guest house. It's bad enough needing earplugs to sleep in the room next to Zerk and Landon."

"Someone's acting cranky without their hyper hippie close by."

"They're talking about releasing him at the end of the week."

"That's great. Sorry I haven't been more of a help."

"Don't even think it, you've got Princess and Juvie covered. So, anything you can think of we need?"

"Give me the list," Brody held out his hand and took the envelope he'd scribbled on, then added to the list. "When are you headed back to the hospital?"

"Probably tomorrow morning, mid-day, they've rescheduled all my appointments, thankfully my clients have been good about it."

"You're one of the best."

"Thanks, I better get this done."

"Oh, I forgot, the kids need juice boxes, Lucky, Princess and Juvie are almost out," Brody called out behind him.

Priest chuckled as he headed back to the grab a cart and get to shopping. It was a bit more expensive than going to the big store about thirty minutes away, but they always preferred to keep things local if they could. They liked Powers just the way it was.

As he slowly filled the cart, he marked things off the paper. A strange tingling started at the base of his skull, the hair felt like it was standing on end like he was being watched. He turned to scan the aisle behind him. He was being stupid, he'd lived on the edge of a breakdown for nearly a week. Starting with almost losing Lucky, finally admitting he wanted to push passed his fear and try for something less than platonic. He loved the crazy man, but he was still scared of ruining what they already had.

He shook his head as he grabbed three gallons of milk to go along with the several boxes of cereal. The crew ate like teenagers. Most afternoons could find the guys standing leaned back against the counter shoveling copious amounts of sugar into their systems. He'd brought green stuff one time, and you'd think he'd brought an infectious disease into the house.

Turning the corner to head for the checkout he bumped someone with the cart.

"Sorry, I didn't—"

Everything inside him froze and his lungs seized as he looked into beautiful hazel eyes that were filled with rage. Andre blocked his way. His hands went sweaty where they had the handle of the cart in a death grip. He felt like he was being choked.

"Hello, Matthew, isn't this a pleasant surprise?"

His panicked gaze darted around in search of help, and that's when he noticed a few familiar men loitering a few aisles down. He couldn't stop his body from shaking as his heart threatened to pound out of his chest.

"Wha-what are—"

"We've come to visit you, you didn't stick around long after your mother's funeral. I didn't get a chance to offer my condolences before your…friend so rudely interrupted me. How is he by the way? If I'm not mistaken I overheard he had an unfortunate accident."

The coldness of Andre's tone and the evil mirth in his eyes caused a thought to form.

"You—"

"Now don't go thinking stupid shit, Matthew, if memory serves it never got you anywhere."

"Priest?"

He almost sighed in relief at the welcome sound of Linus' voice. A gentle touch skimmed his lower back. If anyone other than him had touched him at that moment, he'd have come out of his skin.

"You doing okay," Linus asked.

He turned to give Linus a reassuring smile but froze at the anger showing clearly in eyes very much like Lucky. And he said the first thing that popped into his terror-addled brain. "You finally picked up the horn?" The black glass septum horn was thick in the middle and tapered down to blunt points. It was odd to see Linus looking like, well, them.

"A few days ago, thanks for ordering it. Lou and I saw Lucky's car, no one else would brave driving it. We wanted to take you to dinner tonight."

"We were in the middle—"

Linus snorted to cut Andre off, his arm wrapped around him and he was tugged against the man's side. Linus was taller and slightly broader than his own frame, but the man was all muscle, not a lot of softness. It was strangely comforting.

"I don't give a fuck what you were in the middle of, I'm talking to my brother-in-law. Since he doesn't appear to have shit to say to you, move on and take your lackeys with ya."

"Will finish this later, Matthew."

"Don't even fucking think about it, man, I'm not making an idle threat."

Andre didn't stick around, he nodded to the other men, and they disappeared quickly out of the store. It wasn't until he knew they weren't coming back that his stiff shoulders collapsed and his knees went weak.

"Hey, look at me."

Soft, yet strong hands grabbed his face and lifted him to meet Linus' gaze.

"Deep even breaths, do it with me."

He eventually got his lungs working and mimicked Linus.

"No, don't close your eyes, keep looking at me. That's right, everything is okay. Just you and me," Linus cooed in a soothing tone. "We've got all the time in the world."

He counted the tiny yellow and green specks in Linus' irises. Inhaled the warm scent of coffee-laced breath and eventually, his muscles began to relax. He felt safe, not to the degree that Lucky made him feel, but close.

"You with me?"

He nodded, and Linus studied him for long seconds before he seemed satisfied and released him.

"Something I need to know?"

"That was—"

"The sadistic asshole ex, I figured that part out. Doesn't exactly look like your type. Thought unwashed, dreadlocked hippies were more your kink."

"Lucky isn't unwashed, he always smells like hemp and lemon, with an undertone of musky incense."

"Whatever gets you off."

"What is it with the Trenton's and sex?"

"Naw, you're not lumping me with them. I bring dates around I know will drive them crazy."

"Ah, now I see the method in your madness."

"What can I say, they made me the way I am. Besides, Lou always tries to sleep with the women I bring around, maybe eventually she'll find one of them she likes."

"Weird matchmaking practice."

"I do what I can, so, dinner with us, we'll pick you up at the house at six."

"Will Lily and Damon be there?"

"Nope, just the three of us. Mom's on this damn vegan kick and if we get one more offer of some fucked up tofu loaf we're gonna go insane."

"Maybe learn to cook?"

"What the hell for? That's why they invented takeout. Come on, let's get you through the line and to the car. I'll feel better once I know you're on your way home. Anyone there?"

"It's Trouble's day off, he headed to pick Princess up when I left so he should be back by now."

"You got my number, text when you get there."

"Thank you for what—"

"Don't even try, me and Lucky don't always get along. It's been that way forever, but my brother loves you. You're family even if we're a bit crazy and no one else would want to claim us."

It didn't take long to pay for the groceries and get them to the car. Lou even hugged him before he got in Lucky's car. He pulled off and glanced in the rear view to find Linus and Lou standing together with their shoulders touching. Even though he'd always felt included, it was still weird they'd come to his defense.

That's when the thought which semi-formed came back to him. Would Andre be insane enough to try to kill Lucky? The instant answer was yes, he knew it without a doubt. Knowing Andre was in town made it a certainty. Lucky embarrassed him by knocking him down. Andre never hesitated to claim ownership. With every punch, he'd yelled it. He needed to talk to someone. He pulled into the driveway and then grabbed his phone from his pocket.

He scrolled until he found Scary's number.

"Yeah," Scary's gruff voice answered.

"I think Andre tried to kill Lucky," Priest said it so fast to him it sounded like one word.

"Who the fuck is Andre, and why would he try to kill Lucky?"

"He's my ex, he was abusive and insane. I ran into him at the store."

"Are you home?"

"Yes, I just pulled in. He said something about Lucky's unfortunate accident, but—"

"I'm getting Tank and Elijah, we'll be there soon. Stay the fuck inside and don't open the door. Who's there?"

"Trouble. His truck and bike are here. What about Juvie?"

"She's taking an art class, she'll be there a few more hours. They're doing some kind of exhibit at Heller's Gallery at the end of the month."

"Okay."

"Don't fuck around, Priest, do as I say."

"I promise."

The call disconnected without Scary responding. He got the groceries in the house in record time and was putting them away just as the front door opened.

"Priest," Elijah called out.

"In the kitchen."

"Now tell us what the fuck is going on," Scary ordered as he pulled out a chair for Elijah and another for Tank, then stood behind them with his arms crossed over his massive chest.

He took a deep breath and started from the beginning, things he'd never even told his therapist. Elijah's eyes filled with tears, Tank and Scary seethed. His nightmare played out in full color in his head, and all he wanted was Lucky.

Then an idea hit him, would Lucky still want him when Lucky discovered this was all his fault? The tears flowing down his cheeks sped up, and misery swamped him as the what ifs tortured him.

17 THAT MOTHERFUCKER TRIED TO KILL HIM

The investigators in charge of his crash came by to tell him they found evidence it was a possible hit and run. It really wasn't all that surprising. People don't pay enough attention to motorcycles, one sideswipe and a panicked driver equals them fleeing the scene. They asked him too many questions he couldn't answer. He still didn't remember much after he'd left Elijah's house. He hadn't thought much of the visit or the accident that had brought the cops to his room until the phone call that followed.

That was why Priest was curled into his side. His pretty Bear's eyes were swollen and red from crying. Lou and Linus dropped off a devastated Priest an hour ago. They'd left with a promise one of them would be back in the morning to get him. Priest was too upset to relay what happened, but Elijah called while Tank and Scary angrily growled in the background.

He'd known most of the story, not the details and to be honest, he could've done without those. That sadistic fucker had tried to grab his Priest from the grocery store. If Linus hadn't been there—he didn't want to think about what would've happened.

That motherfucker had tried to kill him, and his man was blaming himself. That wasn't going to fly, and he'd tell Priest as soon as he woke up. He tensed as the door opened, then relaxed as Twitch walked inside.

"Hey, mind a few visitors?"

Twitch was pretty and femme, sweetest guy, but he could get annoying quick.

It was one of the things he liked about the man.

"I brought some dinner. Scary found out Priest didn't eat and it was my turn to cook. I had plenty of leftovers."

"Thanks, who came with you?"

Twitch groaned as rolled his eyes as he looked over his shoulder as the door opened. A blond behemoth walked in, and his huge boots echoed off the walls. Crave couldn't be quiet to save his fucking life.

The young man set the soft cooler on the chair nearest the door.

"Tiptoe, motherfucker, my bear is sleeping," he hissed quietly through clenched teeth.

"I see head trauma didn't improve your disposition. Shame." Crave flopped into a chair beside the bed, and it creaked under his weight.

The man was huge. Looked like a bodybuilder. "Dude, you need to lay off the roids, I heard it shrivels your dick. Rumor is it's almost an innie now."

Twitch giggled quietly as he hoisted himself gently onto the bed. If it wasn't for the man's beautiful looks, he'd swear Twitch tried to make himself as invisible as possible.

Unless he was tending bar, he wore clothes that hung on his slim frame and left his long hair loose to hide his face.

"Fuck you, man, I'm rocking ten inches of prime dick."

"I could've gone without that information." Twitch made gagging noises.

"I hear that a lot." Crave smirked.

"Pig," Twitch whispered with disgust.

"Don't matter the inches if ya can't use it."

"I know exactly how to use it, I've got the men lined up—"

"Shut up, we don't need to hear about your deviant behavior." Twitch reached out and rubbed Lucky's leg in a soothing rhythm.

He was sure it was more for Twitch's benefit than his. The young man was a very tactile person. If Twitch didn't focus, he had a tendency to use people as security blankets. Stroking their arm or hand as he tried to ground himself. It got him in trouble more times than Lucky could count. Crave was in a constant fight on nights Twitch was feeling insecure or overwhelmed. He didn't mind so he let the man do it. Twitch had some of the same coping mechanisms Priest did. So he felt protective of Twitch.

"Could you not rub on everyone you see, fuck, he's taken," Crave rumbled, and anger filled his voice.

Twitch seemed to recoil and moved his hands to his lap.

"Come here." Lucky motioned for Twitch with his good hand and scooted over, opening a bit of space between him and Priest.

"What's wrong," Priest asked in a sleepy voice.

"Twitch needs some TLC." It was all he needed to say because Priest lifted his head. They'd discussed Twitch a time or two after nights at Brawlers. Priest saw some of himself in the younger man.

"You're tiny enough to fit in the space."

"The fuck he is." Crave surged to his feet.

"Shut the fuck up," Lucky hissed.

Twitch hesitated, but Priest leaned up enough to grab his wrist to bring him close to tuck him between them.

"If I knew you were—"

"You don't want to finish that, Crave," Priest threatened then laid back down to lay his arm over both him and Twitch.

It took a lot to piss Priest off. Although he knew Priest was a little raw at the moment and Twitch was a good buffer. Good thing he heard the chair strain under Crave's weight again, or he couldn't guarantee what Priest would do.

"His locs are surprisingly soft."

He heard Priest whisper to Twitch and Lucky smiled as he felt Priest pull one free from the tie to give to Twitch. He felt nothing but friendly affection for Twitch, and he knew Priest understood that.

The three of them ignored Crave's grumbling. He was sometimes a bastard when it came to Twitch, but he knew there was no way Crave had a thing for Twitch. Twitch was the complete opposite of Crave's type. Yeah, Crave liked them submissive, but he also liked them freaky. That wasn't Twitch.

They all fell into silence as Twitch rolled Lucky's dreadlock between his fingers. Priest's breaths started evening out again. Lucky stared up at the ceiling. He didn't know what he was going to do while he was laid up and unable to protect Priest.

"He needs a protection detail," Crave whispered.

It sounded weird since Crave didn't know how to be quiet.

"What do y'all know," he asked.

"Only need to know information. Crazy ex who showed up in town. Eluded—"

"Eluding, do you even know what that means."

Lucky snorted as Crave cursed under his breath. Twitch muffled his own laugh against his chest. It really wasn't wide enough for the three of them, but it was fine.

"Can I continue," Crave asked and continued when Lucky grunted. "As I was saying, apparently the bastard tried to kill you. Not that I don't blame him you're annoying enough to make someone want to murder you. I've thought about it a time or two."

"So, did y'all go over the schedule?"

"Yeah, Psycho's out, he's self-appointed security for Elijah and Juvie. He sticks close to them. He's to call Scary or text Tank with his plans, he'll coordinate with us who's available to send."

"I appreciate this."

"No problem, man, if it was one of our boyfriends or husbands, we'd want the same offer. I need coffee, and I think the cafeteria is still open." Crave pushed up from the chair and headed for the door, light flooded the room, and then it went dark as Crave disappeared.

"I don't want to be a bother, Lucky."

"You're no bother, and until I'm out of here, I want someone to watch you for me. Please do this for me. Andre's a crazy fucker. He ran me off the road and would've taken you if Linus hadn't shown."

"Okay, but I'm here, at home or the shop. It seems an imposition—"

"It's not, Scary and Tank wouldn't have offered. Now get some sleep. Twitch is definitely comfortable." Lucky chuckled at Twitch's soft snores.

Priest laid his head back down and buried his nose in Twitch's long, curly hair. Lucky relaxed into the bed and close his eyes. All the fucked up scenarios played out in his head. Andre repeating with his friends what he'd done before. Priest needing him and him not being able to get to him. He wouldn't survive losing Priest. He'd waited years to get Priest to accept him, to believe he loved him beyond being his best friend.

Everyone else had seen it, commented on it, maybe not in front of Priest, but definitely at his expense. His friends didn't understand it stung like a motherfucker. They would've eventually gotten to this point, and he'd been willing to be patient. His bear needed tenderness and to be loved on. He just wanted to love him, but first, he had to make sure Priest stayed safe.

He still had to show him the cottage where he'd made a home for them to live in even if it had only been as friends. It wasn't much, but it would be theirs.

"I see they're asleep," Crave actually spoke quietly.

He opened his eyes and turned his head to the left. "Priest and Twitch don't sleep a lot."

"How the fuck would you know what Twitch does?"

"Priest and him play some online game, an RPG or something. It passes the time when they can't sleep."

"What else do you know?" Crave leaned forward and rested his thickly veined forearms on his knees.

"If you want to know something ask Twitch instead of being a dick. The guy actually has—feelings. I know strange fucking concept especially with the tricks you pick up."

Crave hand shot out and almost touched his loc to remove it from Twitch's hand.

"Don't take his security. He fucking fine."

"I have to watch his back at work. If he's got shit going on—"

"Whatever he has going on is his business, you can leave. I'll send him home with Priest in the morning."

"Like that would ya, two men on your dick."

He wasn't taking the bait. Crave just wanted to fight. Other than fucking, fighting was the only thing Crave enjoyed. Well, those and making everyone around him as uncomfortable as possible.

"If you're gonna stay, keep quiet and let them sleep. There's a cot over there, curl up and be quiet."

Crave pushed to his feet and stormed across the room. The man liked to be in people's business too much. He had enough shit, he didn't need Crave's too. He wanted to sleep, and he needed to figure out how to get out of there as soon as possible. What he needed more was his and Priest's bed, their crazy fur babies and some pizza—greasy pizza and a beer.

18 WHERE DO YOU WANT THE BODY BURIED

Flowers arrived a week later, Priest stared at the bouquet and knew who they were from even without a card. Andre had picked up flowers the day after every hit and time he'd begged Andre to stop during sex because it hurt. Andre seemed to like it best those nights.

Scary and Tank sat at the table, Elijah perched on Scary's lap with his legs across Tank's thighs. Those three were an odd trio, but they made their relationship work. He wondered what it was like to be so sexually free, so unafraid to be intimate. Sometimes he found himself jealous and wondered if he was keeping Lucky from— Lucky's strong hand took his and gave it a squeeze.

Lucky only came home the day before after spending two weeks in the hospital. He was hobbling around on one crutch and refusing to sit still. It was driving Priest crazy chasing after him.

"Where do you want us to hide the body," Scary asked, and there wasn't an ounce of joking in the question.

"No one is hiding bodies," Priest squeaked.

"He's joking." Elijah shot a fake glare at Scary.

Since Elijah had hooked up with Scary and Tank, the sweet man turned downright vicious. Well, not vicious, he was still nice as fuck, but he stood up for himself. Didn't hurt he had a personal bodyguard. That was still a point of contention between Elijah and his men. Psycho didn't listen to damn word Scary or Tank said.

"No, I wasn't."

Tank snorted and tried to hide it with a cough.

"I'd put you two on the couch, but you two would have too much fun without me."

Lucky let out a loud laugh and Priest choked on the mouthful of water he was about to swallow.

"We have a daughter running around, we wouldn't be having any fun. Don't get any ideas," Scary warned.

"I still think you should go to the cops," Landon suggested as he strode into the room.

"Elijah didn't go to the cops."

"Psycho and Scary dealt out their own brand of justice. Which I'm not condoning." From his smile Elijah totally was. "I think we handle this in-house."

"You're starting to sound like your husbands, it's a bit creepy," Brody said from his seat on the counter with Trouble between his legs and leaned back against his chest.

"It was bound to happen, they're together all the time," Trouble answered as he nuzzled his scruffy cheek to Brody's smooth one.

"So, what are you planning, kidnap him and beat the shit out of him until he agrees to stay away."

"Pretty much," Scary said with a smirk.

"Lucky, don't you have an opinion, you're being way too quiet."

"To be honest, I think we should go to the cops. They already came to the hospital to ask questions since they're treating it as a hit and run. As tempting as seeing that fucker in a deep hole we do anything wrong side of legal and we're fucked."

"True, so calling the cops is the best option."

Priest didn't want to deal with the cops. They'd ask too many questions. Make him feel like shit about not reporting the abuse and rape. Would they even believe him after four years? No one else had, not even his mother.

Lucky used his thumb to rub a soothing circling on the back of Priest's hand. Lucky's silent comfort meant everything to him.

"Detective, this is Lee Trenton, I have new information on the hit and run—" Lucky paused. "Yeah, you can come by, twenty minutes is fine." Lucky disconnected the call and laid his phone on the table.

"We're out." Scary lifted Elijah to his feet.

"Big, bad Scary running from the—"

"Damn right, I got enough shit dealing with those fuckers sitting outside my bar for no fucking reason. At least it's down to one guy. New deputy, never seen him before. Newbie getting all the shit jobs."

"He's pretty though," Elijah confessed and snorted as Scary and Tank rumbled.

"Didn't think pretty did it for ya." Scary smacked Elijah's ass.

"It doesn't, but I can notice. We'll see you later. Juvie's about done with her art class. We're late, and she starts to worry."

He watched the trio leave with Psycho close behind. That one he couldn't figure out. Psycho shadowed Elijah and Juvie wherever they went. The only time Psycho remained behind was when Elijah went to work.

The rest started filing out to give them privacy for when the detective arrived. He knew the guys didn't like new people in their space. Most of them didn't have any fans in law enforcement. It wasn't like they were criminals, but appearance was enough to get them noticed. They wanted to go back to their lives as much as he did. If and when that would happen still remained a mystery.

"It'll be okay." Lucky tugged him onto his lap.

He soaked in Lucky's warmth and the comforting scents which were all Lucky.

"I just want it over with. Get back to life as usual."

"It will, we gotta get this fucker off our backs first and then I have a surprise for you."

"You finally going to let me see," he asked.

He didn't have to specify. He was dying to see the house Lucky bought. When they'd move in was a mystery, and he'd miss Twirled House, this was the place he'd finally started to feel safe. He was probably planning too far in advance, but it was a nice dream. A home of his own with Lucky and their crazy pets, Princess and Juvie spending nights and who knows maybe he wanted more. The thought of more still terrified him.

"I sent someone to clean it up a bit. It's been about a month since I sneaked away to take care of the place."

"You keeping secrets. It seems weird. What else have you kept from me?" Even though he didn't want to sound defensive, the question came across as an accusation. He stood to throw the flowers in the trash, but Lucky's hands on his hips kept him from walking away.

"That I've loved you forever. You were it when I met you." Lucky leaned in and pressed his face to the curve of Priest's stomach.

He cringed a bit, but his muscles under his soft stomach contracted. It was a strange rippling that worked its way into his chest. He almost felt like he couldn't catch his breath.

"I love how soft you are." Lucky slipped just his fingertips beneath his shirt.

The cast on Lucky's left hand was rough against his skin.

"Six packs—"

"Whoever says this isn't sexy as fuck, is crazy."

This time he held his breath as Lucky's nosed the bottom of his t-shirt up to place a nipping kiss on his hairy belly right above his navel. He was hairier than he'd been after years of waxing and shaving, he'd put back on the weight he'd lost from starving to fit Andre's idea of what Priest should be.

"He doesn't belong here," Lucky hissed as he tugged Priest's waistband.

He stumbled and then came to rest astride Lucky's thighs.

"You have to be careful, you've got broken bones and just because you had Laparoscopic surgery doesn't mean you can just—"

A rough kiss cut him off, and Lucky slanted his mouth across his nipping sharply at his lips.

"This is you and me, I won't have that bastard of an ex ruining us. I'm fine. Just can't wait to get the casts off, but if you're gentle, we can fool around. Ya know ya want this sexy hippie."

Priest sucked his lips between his teeth to hide the smile, but he couldn't help snorting out a laugh as Lucky waggled his thick, dark blond brows.

"You're so damn weird."

"And you love me for it."

"Yes."

"Yes, what?" Lucky's voice dropped to an almost dangerous rumble.

Something flared in his gaze Priest had never seen before. He didn't know if it excited or terrified him.

"Say it, Priest, tell me." The demand was clear.

"I love you."

"Fuck yes, I love you so much."

The kiss Lucky gave him was very much like their first real one in the hotel room. Desperation mixed with a teasing retreat and advance. He slipped his arms around Lucky's neck, tangled his fingers in the man's thick locs as the tip of Lucky's tongue danced over the seam of his mouth. He tentatively parted his lips, and his tongue peeked out. Together they groaned as their tongues touched and Lucky took over thrusting inside. The depth of his desire shocked him, and he hugged Lucky closer. The softness of his stomach and chest conforming to the hard planes of Lucky's body.

An ache began in his balls, and his dick began to harden. He shivered as Lucky clutched at his back and his fingertips dug deep into Priest's skin. His hips involuntarily jerked, and he rubbed against the deep ridges of Lucky's abs.

"You're so beautiful, all mine, no one will ever see you like this." Lucky bit at his bottom lip. "All flushed and turned on. Eyes all fucking wild. Your body needing only mine. Say it, Priest, say you're mine—always."

He felt like he was coming out of his skin. His muscles quivered, and he was so close to coming in his jeans. It wasn't like any of the times he tried to jerk off. The frustration at a body he couldn't make feel.

"Say it, baby, let me hear it, please."

It was Lucky's please, the edge of pleading to it.

"Yours, always, since the first night you let me sleep with you. So safe—" His words ended on a sob.

He wanted and needed things he couldn't understand. Sex had always been pain and humiliation. What the fuck was this?

"This is me loving on you. No pain. I'll never hurt you. You're always in control. What happens or doesn't happen is up to you."

"But that isn't fair—"

"It is fair, your choice, when you're ready and if you're never ready I'll always be right here. Okay," Lucky asked.

He didn't understand how a man who embraced his sexuality would easily give up a normal sex life to be with him. Intimacy was one thing. The kisses and cuddling, touches Lucky so freely gave, he could accept those, but could he open his body completely to Lucky?

Lucky placed tiny, sweet kisses all over his face.

"I know what you're thinking and what we do, how we decide to show physical love is our business, no one needs to know or approve. I want every inch of you. However, I can—"

A loud rapping at the back patio door made them turn to find two men in suits with disapproving expressions, one even bordered on disgust.

"Let's talk to these assholes and tomorrow we'll go see our house. It's about time you decided how the hell you want it decorated. I sort of took liberties."

"I'm sure you did."

"One more kiss, they can turn away if they don't fucking like it."

He probably gave in too easily, but he craved one more kiss before his past took away their moment. Another loud series of knocks broke them apart, and he eased off Lucky's lap to go answer the door. He was about to rip open a wound he'd left festering too long, and he was ready for it to be over. Starting to plan his future and stop living in the past was his top priority because it's what Lucky and him deserved.

19 THE COTTAGE

Nerves twisted his sore gut, and he swore he was close to puking. Until the turn off to get to the cottage he'd bought less than a mile outside of Powers, he'd been fine. Now all he could think was Priest was going to hate it. He should have bought it with Priest and not assumed like he always did. What the fuck had he been thinking?

"Are you going to puke?"

He didn't appreciate Priest's obvious amusement at his rare show of nerves. With his over-inflated confidence and his radical honesty upbringing made second guessing himself so rare until recently he couldn't remember a time he had.

"Not funny, what if you hate it? We can sell—"

A loud gasp and a slamming of the brakes had Lucky's body weight pulling at his seatbelt. He shot a look forward to see what had Priest's face ashen. Had Andre found them, but all he saw was the cottage.

"Great, Mama had the Model T delivered." Flowers flowed from the bed of the truck. Lily promised to have all the landscaping done before he got out of the hospital. A rope swing hung from the only towering tree near the house.

Priest was quiet except for small hitches in his breathing. He turned his head to find tears dotting Priest's thick lashes.

"Hey, what's wrong, we can change—"

"It's perfect. Can I go inside," Priest asked in a voice that was too quiet.

"Of course, it's ours, here." He pulled the single key from his pocket and held it out to Priest.

The man's strong hands shook as he took them and then drove forward until he parked in front of the white picket fence.

He snorted as he saw the mailbox with The Trenton's written in his mother's beautiful handwriting. Point to his Mama on her plan to get herself a son-in-law. They'd never talked about marriage. As far as he knew, Priest didn't believe in it and he wasn't sure he did either. A signed piece of paperwork didn't always mean two people loved each other.

Priest was already out of the car, and he opened his own door as he struggled his one crutch from the backseat. He kept a close eye on Priest as Lucky made his way out of the car and followed at a slow pace. Priest touched everything as he passed. The pointed tips of the fence, the sun-warmed metal of the mailbox and Priest fumbled a bit with the gate latch.

After the police interview and all he had to confess, Priest had seemed on edge. Maybe seeing the cottage was a little more overwhelming than he'd anticipated. It could've waited a few more days, but Priest was determined to see it today.

He wanted to ask questions and to know what was going on in Priest's head, but he bit the inside of his cheek to keep quiet.

The Mosaic tiles of recycled colored glass made up the walkway. Priest stopped to cast his gaze downward and turned as Priest took it all in. Instead of pale, Priest's face was flushed, and a small half-smile tilted his mouth.

His tense muscles relaxed at the wonder and happiness in front of him. Priest turned, and his steps quickened as he approached the small porch and ascended the three steps.

He heard the snick of the lock, but Priest didn't go inside.

"Are you okay," Lucky asked as he climbed slowly to the landing and stopped behind Priest.

"I'm just trying to imagine what the inside looks like."

"You don't have to imagine, you can just go inside."

"I can't believe you did all this for me."

"For us." He stepped forward and leaned down slightly to rest his chin on Priest's shoulder. "There's three bedrooms, not huge or anything, but I wanted you to have your own room if you—"

"You don't want to sleep with me here?"

"Are you crazy, I can't barely sleep without you. No way in fuck I'm gonna give up you sleeping beside me, but I wanted you to have a—"

"Choice," Priest finished for him. "No matter how pushy you can be, you've always given me options. I could always say no."

"Of course, you have the right to say no any damn time you want. I'd never take that away."

"Thank you."

It was all Priest said before he opened the door and pushed it open. Priest stood on the threshold, almost seeming frozen there until he took a hesitant step forward. Lucky followed but stepped to the side and leaned back against the wall. Except for bedrooms and baths, it was open, he'd added large picture windows that let in the sunlight.

"The furniture was used, but I reupholstered and stripped and finished everything. It took forever to redo the hardwood floors. You can change anything you want."

"No," Priest practically yelled. "It's fucking perfect. Everything is just right."

He upholstered the ceilings in midnight fabric with tiny mirrors that would twinkle when they caught the firelight or the night lights he'd plugged in. Priest didn't like anything to be in complete darkness.

"Show me everything." Priest practically danced in place with excitement.

"As you can see this is the living room, and the kitchen is right there. There's a half bath off the kitchen, a full one at the end of the hall and one in the master bedroom." He placed the crutch under his arm and limped forward until he could take Priest's hand.

He led him toward the narrow hallway. All the doors were open to show sparsely furnished guest rooms. The bathroom that they'd already stocked with everything. He got a bit nervous when he reached their room. Unlike the other rooms, that one was closed.

"Go ahead, open it." He stepped to the side to let Priest take his spot.

Priest turned the old brass knob and opened the door. A huge four-post bed stood in the center of the room.

Colorful printed Saris were tied and draped around the dark wood to pool on the dark purple carpet. Priest had a fondness for purple.

"This is our room," Priest asked.

"Yeah, go on, again everything was used, but Mama and me spent a lot of time refinishing everything."

"Can we stay here tonight?"

"Yeah, the bathroom's stocked with all your favorite things. I didn't know if you wanted to, but I had Trouble sneak groceries and our backpacks into the trunk. I thought maybe you'd like a little time away. They don't expect us back for a few days."

He suddenly had an armful of shaking, beautiful man.

"Thank you," Priest repeated between quick kisses as smiling lips pushed against his.

He couldn't contain his smile. He'd done this fucking right at least.

"Think I did okay, huh?"

"You did perfect, this is ours, I'll have to pay half the mortgage."

"No mortgage, ours free and clear. Mama and Dad set up funds when we were kids for us to travel the world, plan coups or you know go to college."

"You used that money to buy us a house?"

"Yeah, it seemed like the perfect plan for it. There's still a bit left over. Dad used his trust fund from a grandfather he'd never met to set it up, and they added a bit over the years, not much. A professor and a crazy woman aren't exactly rich."

Priest laughed as he'd intended.

"I can't believe you used your coup funding money for this."

"What else would I have used it for. We got pets together. We made our relationship all official and shit. A house was the next step. I'd hoped I hadn't fucked it up."

"No, you definitely didn't fuck it up. I'm going to go get our stuff. I'll be right back, I can't believe you—"

"It's ours, I have the papers for you to sign in my pack. Once you sign, if you want to sign."

"I'll be right back."

He chuckled to himself as Priest ran from the room. His heavy boots echoing on the wood floors.

Part of him never thought they'd be there together. He'd made a will at the same time he named Priest his power of attorney. It would've been Priest's no matter what. He wanted to take care of the man he'd never thought he'd have beyond the strength of their friendship.

If security and safety were all he'd had the ability to give Priest, then he wanted to do anything within his power to make it happen.

Priest calling his name drew him from his thoughts, but he stayed beside the door. He closed his eyes to listen to Priest move around the kitchen. After a few minutes, he heard Priest returning to the bedroom. Priest walked through the door, headed for the bed to set their bags on the mattress.

"You know the kitchen is stocked with enough food for a week."

"Mama, I called her yesterday to let her know we were coming out here."

"She has a key?"

"She shouldn't, she was going to leave it in the cabinet before she left."

"Can we take a nap?"

"Anything you want." Lucky pushed away from the wall and approached his side of the bed. He scooted onto the bed and tried to take his shoe off.

"I've got it."

He laid back on the bed as Priest worked on taking off his sneaker and sock. The firm mattress was fucking amazing, and it got even better when Priest was curled up beside him. Priest's head rested on his chest, and his arm slung across Lucky's stomach. He closed his eyes as a throw was pulled up over them. They both stayed silent and as he heard Priest's breathing even out, Priest's big body completely relaxed. He let himself drift off to sleep content.

20 COULD HE BE LOVED?

One night in the cottage turned into three and Priest couldn't bring himself to leave just yet. They'd gone to work and done all the responsible adult things, but instead of going back to Twirled House they'd come home to the cottage each night. Plague and Cyclops found their favorite spot in a cushy bed beside the fireplace.

Lucky was off for a doctor's appointment and was hoping to get a walking cast, so that left him home alone. He received a call earlier that Andre was picked up and taken in for questioning. They'd found paint from Lucky's bike and helmet on the bumper of Andre's rental car.

It was one thing to think the bastard tried to kill Lucky, but another to have proof.

It was the first he'd been alone in a long time. Someone was always around Twirled House or at the shop, Lucky and him were attached at the hip most days and nights. He'd thought a lot, Andre was likely going to jail, and that old ghost of his abusive ex was gone.

For the first time in his life, he felt free and happy. Not that he wasn't before. Lucky, his friends and chosen family made him happy, especially Lucky.

He added a bit more Sandalwood and Ginger bubble bath to the steaming water. It was weird, but he thought his best in a bath. He stepped into the water and laid his head back against the rim, once the water covered him to his chin he turned the taps with his toes. The waves of his hair stuck to his wet face and he closed his eyes.

Could he be loved? He knew Lucky loved him. It existed in the way Lucky treated him and respected his boundaries. He wanted to know if he could accept physical love. They hadn't repeated what happened at the hotel or in the kitchen the week before. It was the same as always, Lucky touched him as if he just needed to know Priest was really there. Lucky cuddled him on the couch or in bed, kissing his brow or the top of his head.

He felt desire, but he didn't know what to do about it, and that bothered him. He was terrified his mind and body would betray him. Lucky said it didn't matter, but he was sexually attracted to Lucky and wanted to try.

Lifting his hand, he stroked his palm across his chest, and he let out a shuddered breath as the slight calluses rubbed his nipple. The beaded point caught on his skin. Nerves tightened his stomach as he wrapped his free hand around his soft cock. He felt tears leak from the corner of his eyes as his lack of response.

Determined to feel something close to the pleasure Lucky gave him just with a touch, he pulled his dick in slow strokes.

"Priest, enjoying your—"

He wanted to die from embarrassment. He quickly covered his cock with both hands. Never once had he been completely naked in front of Lucky or anyone for that matter. He refused to open his eyes.

"Baby." Lucky's voice sounded in his ear.

He nearly jumped out of his skin.

"You're crying."

Lucky kissed the corner of his eye, and even if the proof was slowly seeping from under his closed lids, he didn't want to admit it.

"What's wrong, tell me," Lucky whispered.

"I—I can't—"

He couldn't finish, and he turned away as misery swamped him taking his ability to speak. How pathetic he couldn't even jerk off? The one thing he could do to bring himself sexual pleasure, to come and he couldn't even do that.

"I know you can, remember the kitchen. You moved those hips and rubbed that cock of yours against my stomach. Come on, I want to try something."

He opened his eyes to see Lucky standing, a soft cast around his wrist. Lucky plucked a towel from the hook beside the tub then held it out in front of him. He kept his dick covered with one hand as he got to his feet, he pulled the stopper with his toes. Stepping out of the tub he stood in front of Lucky, and the taller man wrapped the soft fabric around him.

The rub of the cotton and Lucky's fingertips against his skin caused desire to build. His dick hardened slightly under his hand. He moaned as he leaned his body toward Lucky.

Lucky's hands fisted in the towel and started tugging him out into the bedroom.

"Now, stand right there. You don't have to touch me. Just watch." Lucky released the towel.

It fell to pool at Priest's feet, and he did as Lucky said. Lucky slowly removed his clothes. It was as if he had all the time in the world. Lucky wasn't groping him or leering. He didn't feel threatened. It was safe and comforting and arousing. His chest rose and fell with his quickened breathing.

Warm, smooth tanned skin appeared as each item of Lucky clothes fell to join the towel. He couldn't resist staring as Lucky's hard cock jutted out from a thick nest of blond pubes. The thick ring of Lucky's Prince Albert glinted in the soft light of the bedside lamp.

"See what you do to me. How fucking hard you make me?" Lucky punctuated his words with quick strokes along his veined shaft. "Do you remember the workshop?"

He nodded his head.

"I'm going to sit on the bed. You're going to sit on my lap. Nothing more."

Lucky's voice was soft and soothing as Lucky climbed onto the bed, his foot with the walking cast stretched out while he crossed the other under his injured one.

He swallowed around the growing lump in his throat as he did as Lucky asked. Lucky held his cock against his stomach. He sat in the cradle of his thighs, slid his arms over Lucky's shoulders. When his dick rested alongside Lucky's, he moaned at the feel of hot silky skin and body warmed metal.

"Now, you're in control," Lucky whispered.

Lucky's mouth was against his, their lips brushing with each word and breath.

"What do I—"

"Do what you want. Touch me anyway, anywhere."

He'd slept beside a shirtless Lucky plenty of times, even a naked Lucky a time or two when he'd first taken to sleeping in Lucky's bed. His dick thickened, and he looked down. Lucky's cock was longer, but not as thick as his own, the skin darker. The foreskin pulled back to expose the flush glistening head. He wasn't ready to touch there just yet.

Instead, he spread his hands and massaged the hard pecs, Lucky's pebbled nipples and traced the indents of Lucky's cut to perfection abs. Lucky wasn't bulky or hairy, his skin soft and littered with scars both faded and new.

Lucky gasped, and Priest realized Lucky shook hard under his touch. Lucky's body became slick with sweat. His cheeks flushed red along his high cheekbones. He noticed Lucky's good hand was fisted in the covers.

"Is this okay?" He grew insecure. Why wasn't Lucky touching him? Holding him like he'd done at the workshop?

"Tell me I can touch you?" Lucky's voice was rough and pitched low as if he were afraid to scare him off.

He started to nod, but Lucky shook his head.

"No, I need to hear you say it."

Lucky was giving him his choices back. The ones that were repeatedly taken from him. His cock jerked at the power he felt. Someone confident and strong was relinquishing control to him.

"Yes."

It was apparently all Lucky needed to hear because the next second Lucky's mouth was on his. Kissing him tenderly, but there was an intensity—an overwhelming pleasure he hadn't expected. He couldn't be still as Lucky's hands traveled every inch he could reach. He tensed as Lucky gripped his ass and he waited, but the man didn't push into his crease just tugged him forward.

He held his breath as their cocks were trapped between their bellies. Sweat ran down the indent of his spine, at his temples and gathered in the hair on his chest. They came together in slow, rhythmic rocks and swivels of their hips. The kiss didn't end until they both were fighting for breath.

It was all slow, sensual movements—no hurry to the finish. His whole body thrummed with pleasure. Long, slender fingers sunk into his hair and pulled his head back, and Lucky's tongue teased the indent at the base of his throat.

"S'fucking beautiful, taste so—" Lucky sucked at his throat.

One of Lucky's hands remained in his hair and the other curved around his waist. His body bowed as he rutted against Lucky's stomach. He was so close. His cock and balls ached with the need to come. It was just there out of reach as if he were waiting for something.

"I've thought about this so fucking—"

"What did you think about?" He didn't know where he got the brain cells to ask.

"You, watching you, s'many times, come for me, Priest." Lucky licked up this side of his throat.

He felt lips and teeth tugging at his earlobe as he worked himself against Lucky's abs.

"Love you." Lucky moaned into his ear.

His balls tightened and his cock pulsed as he came over Lucky's stomach. His movements jerky. Blood roared in his ears. He called Lucky's name over and over as strong arms hugged him tightly.

His eyes flew open as Lucky leaned back. Lucky grabbed his dick using his come to smooth the way. Lucky's eyes shimmered, and his body was drenched in sweat as he stroked his dick in an almost brutal pace. His man's stomach was drawn in tight as Lucky curled, his lips were parted and swollen. Lucky's locs wild behind him.

"Touch me, please, fuck." Lucky's dick was flushed, and beads of pre-come slid down the shaft.

The sound wet and dirty as Lucky jerked harder and faster. His moans were desperate and needy.

He felt turned on and helpless at the same time as Lucky writhed beneath him. Lucky's movements strong enough to lift him as the man strove for release.

"Where—"

Lucky's casted hand nudged his until it slipped between their bodies. His eyes widened, and nervousness settled in his chest, like a panic attack but not. He shifted backward, and his tentatively touched Lucky's hole, felt the hair circling it and he massaged around it. Felt the clench of the muscle.

"Fuck, Priest, finger fucked myself." The tendons and muscles strained in Lucky's neck as he threw his head back, "Thinking, came S'fucking hard."

His dick jerked and tried to harden again at the confession.

"S'sexy, you topping me."

He leaned down to push his mouth against Lucky's as he used his thumbnail to tug at Lucky's Guiche. A high-pitch whine shocked him, and he pushed too hard, fingertips popping inside, and Lucky's body bowed as wet heat painted his belly and cock. Their bodies covered in come and sweat, Lucky trembling and gasping for breath.

They whispered their love between kisses and promises of forever.

Everyone thought his Lucky was crazy, but to him the hyper hippie was everything. His comfort. His safety. His home.

EPILOGUE: MARRY ME?

Three months later...

The spot on the bed beside him was cold, and he fucking hated waking up without Priest. He rolled from bed—the air cool on his naked skin as he strode toward the kitchen.

"What the hell are you doing up," Lucky barked out as he walked around the corner.

"Well, hello, son, someone really needs to work on his personal grooming."

He groaned at his dad's amused voice.

"What the fuck are you doing here and where is my pretty bear?"

"Housewarming cookout, remember?"

"That's today?" Why didn't Priest remind him of these things?

His dad tossed him a hand towel, and he caught it.

"Yeah, and Priest is in the backyard with everyone else. Princess and Juvie are running around, and they really don't need to see that."

"It's too early for this shit, and I had plans today," He hollered over his shoulder as he headed back to the bedroom.

With pissed off movements he threw on jeans and a threadbare t-shirt.

"So, do you have the ring?"

"Of course, I've got the ring. You two gave it to me, remember?"

He needed a lot of caffeine. He reached into the very back of his top drawer and pulled out the box in Priest's favorite shade of purple. His parents had kept it safe for the past year, and he'd asked for it last week at family dinner. So, he'd gotten a little ahead of himself with the whole let me buy a ring and a house thing, but that shit was inevitable. Priest was his. He'd known his whole life he'd been waiting for someone, just hadn't known exactly who until he'd seen Priest for the first time.

"Is Mama ready to officiate this fucker?"

"She's been ready since you brought Priest to dinner the first time. Don't you think you should have an engagement?"

"Why? I love him, he loves me, we've got furry kids and a house. Still working on Lou renting some womb space because I swear I'm getting a mini-version of Priest running around. And except for the tits and cooch, she looks just like me, but I'd prefer if he or she looks like Priest."

"And if I remember Priest keeps telling you no." His dad chuckled as he plopped on the side of the bed.

"He just doesn't think I'm serious. How fucking great would it be to have this beautiful little version Priest?"

"You know you look way too damn cranky to be getting ready to propose to your soul—"

The sound of glass breaking had him jerking his attention to the door to find Priest frozen in the doorway.

"Fuck, just fucking great, motherfucker!" Lucky tugged roughly at his locs.

"I'm out, I'll keep everyone outside." His dad ran from the room like his ass was on fire.

Suddenly the door slammed, and Priest was leaning against it. He couldn't tell what Priest was thinking.

"I was bringing you coffee."

"Thanks."

"What's that?" Priest motioned towards the box. "Something for me?"

"Um, if you want it."

"You gonna ask me whatever or just keep standing there."

Priest still wasn't showing his hand, and that made him nervous as fuck. He sighed heavily and walked across the room, he fell to his knees.

"Most people think I'm crazy as fuck and should really shut up. I got weird family who aren't any prize..." The box hinges creaked as it opened. "But I was really hoping you liked me enough to, ya know?"

"I know what?"

"Don't be an ass, marry me."

"Wow, I'm overwhelmed."

Lucky leaned his forehead against Priest's belly.

"I had a whole speech planned. A day in bed. Dinner. And then we'd go for a ride out to the lake at Tank's cabin. Now it's all fucked up. I'm sorry."

"Can I even see it?"

Lucky didn't look up as he lifted the opened box. He knew it wasn't much and was probably weird. He'd had it hand carved from an amethyst geode. The band swirled with purples and brilliant white.

"Lucky, this—"

He leaned back and gazed up to find Priest staring at the ring.

"I knew you were mine the minute you walked into the shop that first day. You looked so nervous, and all I wanted to do was hold and touch you. Make you smile. I want to always make you feel safe. I love you, and I want you to wear the ring I had made for you."

The silence drew out, and the longer Priest didn't speak the more he wanted to just curl into a ball on the floor, maybe cry, but only when no one was around.

"Yes, to it all."

Lucky surged to his feet and threw his arms around Priest, then realized what the man said.

"All, what all?"

"Marriage and if you can ever talk your sister into womb space, which I think is a—"

"I got womb room for one," Lou yelled through the door. "None of that freaky twin shit. Fetal Cannibalism freaks me out."

"Score, you were always my favorite womb mate I didn't absorb," he yelled through the door.

"I'll get everyone in line, no sex until after the vows, sinners." Her voice disappeared down the hall.

"So, Mama is ready to marry us."

"Now?"

"Yes. Now, what are we waiting on? Will your decision to marry me change in a month, six months, we're not waiting a year."

"Okay."

"You won't regret it."

He slammed his mouth against Priest's, then pulled away to grab his hand and drag him to the backyard before the man smartened up and changed his mind. He paused in the kitchen and turned to look at Priest.

"I love you, always have."

"Ditto."

"Ditto, really, we've reached the ditto stage?"

"Shut up, Lucky, let's get married."

"Okay."

They walked out into the backyard to rounds of applause and a lot of muttering of about damn time. Priest was his everything, the one he'd been destined for, and he'd never fuck that up.

THE END

ABOUT THE AUTHOR

By day, J.M. is an introverted cook hiding out in her kitchen in the middle of nowhere Ohio, by night and any free time she may have, she is a writer of mainly LGBTQ Fiction and Erotica. Although. she's equal opportunity when it comes to telling a story, she'll even write a bit of straight erotic romance when the mood strikes.

She has been writing for years in old notebooks. At the age of eight, she wrote the worst poem in the history of poetry, but it sparked her love for writing. She reads too much and loves to get lost in other worlds and her favorite stories have to include laughter and having the reader doing at least one double take. Thirty-something, forever restless she uses her stories to ground herself, and find her place of peace.

WHERE TO FIND J.M.
www.jmdabneyauthor.com

AVAILABLE NOW

CRAVE
Brawlers Book 1

Welcome to Brawlers Bar

A quick pit stop for a comfortable bed to sleep turned into an eight-year stay. Vincent "Crave" Butler hit the road the day after college graduation and hadn't looked behind him since. He'd swore to never stop moving, but the night he drove into Powers, Georgia changed the course of his life. He'd hit a bar called Brawlers with its rundown exterior and pride flag beside the door, the next day he had a job. Second in command to the Head of Brawler security, Crave found the place he didn't have to run from. No one would call Crave sane. He lived to make people as uncomfortable as possible just for his own twisted amusement. That all changed when a certain cute as fuck bartender walked in for an interview.

No one wanted Twitch Harrison around. He was small, femme and annoying on his best days, downright abhorrent on his bad ones. When college turned out to be a no-go, and the parents canceled his credit cards he'd needed a job. Walking into Brawlers, the roughest gay bar in his hometown, was like a game of pick the thing that didn't belong—him. The two owners, Scary and Tank, hired him on and four years later he was still that thing that didn't belong. No one made it more apparent than bouncer Crave Butler who didn't hide the fact he barely tolerated Twitch's presence.

Crave threatened every man who thought they'd get the pretty Twitch but would Twitch rather be in their beds than his? Only one way to find out and he hoped Twitch was ready for forever because that's what Crave was determined to have.

✦ ✦ ✦

1 SADLY ALL HIS BRAINS WERE IN HIS DICK

Chaos reigned at Brawlers Bar. Fists flew from every direction and bodies fell against Crave Butler. He was about to spin to take on the guy at his six but pulled the punch at the last moment as Bull his coworker came into view.

"Motherfucker, are all your brains in your fucking dick," Bull growled.

He protested, "This wasn't my fault." He ruined the innocent tone as he laughed like a maniac.

He hadn't thrown the first fucking punch, so actually, he wasn't lying. Bodies started flying up and out of the crowd as he spotted Psycho tossing people around like they weighed nothing. Almost seven-feet of pissed off man was downright fucking Scary; no way in fuck he'd admit that to anyone, though.

Then the realization came. Shit, Psycho was after him. He started to duck and weave, disappearing for someone Crave's size was impossible. He lifted weights at least three times a week, he was the shortest of Brawlers Security team at six-two but other than Psycho he was definitely the bulkiest in muscle mass.

"Elijah is fine," he yelled and tried to hide behind Bull.

"I told you no fights when my pretty boss is in-house."

Crave rolled his eyes, he swore Psycho had a massive hard-on for Elijah. If true, Psycho had a death wish.

"Scary and Tank—"

"Not my bosses. Now, come here so I can kick your ass."

"Bull, do something." Crave peeked over Bull's shoulder. "The fucker is insane."

"Just take it like a man, Crave." Bull walked away.

Crave was exposed. "Come on, man, I didn't throw—"

He ducked a right jab but grunted when a left hook landed against his ribs "Motherfucker, are you wearing brass?" The question ceased when huge hands grabbed his shoulders and pushed him down. Psycho's knee came toward his nose in slow motion. He barely pushed himself out of the way, and the worn denim of Psycho's jeans grazed his cheek.

"Psycho," Elijah's raised voice came out of nowhere.

He turned his head in time to see Elijah with his hands on his hips and a dark brow raised.

"Yes, boss?"

"What are you doing?"

"Kicking Crave's ass."

Crave rolled his eyes as he took advantage of Psycho's distraction and tried to pull away only to earn himself a sucker punch to the gut. The air whooshed from his lungs as he planted his hands on his knees and tried to draw in a breath.

"And why are you kicking Crave's ass?"

"Because he didn't listen to me," Psycho answered.

"Is that a question or an answer?"

"Um, it's an answer, he didn't listen and put you in danger."

Crave snorted. Elijah might be lacking in muscle and height, but the man could wield a mean bat when the time arose.

"I was perfectly safe, Psycho, what have we talked about?"

"Don't beat up on people weaker than—"

Elijah had the nerve to laugh. Bastard.

"No, what did we discuss?"

"To think before we punch, but I thought about it. And after careful consideration, he deserved the beating."

"Psycho."

The big bastard exhaled heavily and hung his head.

"We don't fight with friends. He's not my friend."

"Psycho, come on, let's have another talk, come on." Elijah held out his hand.

Crave straightened and earned an elbow to the gut. "Dammit."

"Psycho, no, bad Psycho, are we going to have to talk about another visit to the doctor?"

Psycho huffed and Crave watched him walk away.

"No, boss, I'm—" Psycho growled, then cleared his throat, "Sorry."

"Shouldn't you tell Crave you're sorry too?"

"Do I have'ta?"

"No, but we still have to talk, buy me a coffee."

Elijah was insane, he'd thought it when the cute man hooked up with his bosses Tank and Scary, but when he adopted Psycho, it turned into a fact. The small man slipped his arm through Psycho's and led him away. Crave breathed a sigh of relief and jumped back as a massive fist came back to pop him in the nuts.

"Dude, that's low."

"What did you do?"

"Nothing, boss."

Psycho smirked over his shoulder as he walked away with Elijah on his arm.

"Your boss won't always be around to save your ass," Crave called out and grimaced as he ducked away as Psycho tried to turn back to him.

"He's gonna kill you one of these days."

Scary's gruff voice made him turn his head to see his boss's amused expression.

"Why haven't you fired his oversized ass yet?"

"Elijah loves that man like a son, which is weird as fuck since the man is only a year younger than him."

"Does he join—"

"I'll kick your ass if you finish that shit right there. I don't know what the fuck is going on with you, but you cause one more fight in my bar, I'll let Psycho kick your ass to the door. Got me?"

"Sorry, man, I shouldn't have said that."

"Damn right," Scary growled and headed toward where Elijah and Psycho were sitting at the bar.

Fuck, Crave slid his hands into his back pockets and watched as Bull cleared the mess. Setting some of Psycho's casualties up with a free round. He probably deserved the beating Elijah saved him from, but he probably needed one from Scary too. Crave lived with a constant inappropriate comment fighting to get free from his mouth. He knew it, and mostly he didn't give a fuck if it got him in trouble, but he knew better than to try his shit with Scary. That mean fucker would hide his body and never think twice.

Scanning the crowd, he noticed most of the rowdy crowd departed. He made his way outside to take his usual spot on a barstool beside the door.

He stared out across the parking lot to the deputy vehicle in the empty lot on the other side of the road. He gave the guy a two-finger salute, and the deputy flashed his headlights. The new guy seemed cool enough. He didn't fuck with them as much as the others did.

He yelled as a bag of ice slammed into his sore stomach. "What the fuck, man." Crave turned his head to find Twitch standing next to him. The man tucked his long curls behind his small ears and crossed his arms over his thin chest. Crave never met a man he'd consider beautiful before, but that ended the minute Twitch sashayed into Brawlers for an interview.

"You pissed off the bosses again."

"Don't fucking start, Twitch."

"I'm not starting anything. Just saying."

"Am I fired?"

They'd threatened to fire him before and with any other job he'd taken he hadn't given a shit about it, but he loved working there.

"They finally have a solid crew they trust, but whatever's going on in that head of yours, you better work it out before they change their minds."

It's like none of them knew him. He was the same as he was the minute he'd walked into Brawlers. Eight years he'd worked the door of Brawlers as second in command to Tank. Like the rest of the crew except the bosses, he'd taken up residence in Bull's house. They lived and worked together sooner or later shit was going to get tense, they'd fight and be done. He had to admit his head was fucked up lately. Crave remembered the minute shit went fucking nuclear—Twitch had smiled at him.

"I ain't got shit going on in my head," he lied like a motherfucker. "And I didn't throw the first punch."

"You rarely do, but you sure as hell don't back down."

"Kinda my job."

"I'm going back inside, Hunter isn't screwing up my paperwork again. How fucking hard is it to learn the POS?"

Twitch didn't wait for him to answer and headed back through the open door. Crave dropped the bag of ice to the ground. He hadn't gotten laid in almost a year, and it was all Twitch's fault. His usual type was a big and muscular, but submissive.

Twitch was too fragile for him, yet he didn't want anyone else. Okay, he hadn't turned into a monk since he'd first laid eyes on Twitch. The unfamiliar guilt he had over the men he'd brought home or hooked up with caused him to hook up infrequently until it ceased completely last summer. He loved sex. Fuck, he just missed fucking, but he only wanted one man.

He'd wanted to touch Twitch's smooth tanned skin and trace every inch of that beautiful slim body from the second Crave had spotted him. Crave dreamed of tangling Twitch's long dark hair around his fist as he fucked Twitch's tight, rounded ass till Twitch screamed for him. He wanted to own Twitch; the man's pleasure and pain all his.

Crave didn't understand the concept of jealousy and didn't become attached, but every man who even looked at Twitch got a warning. With his size, they never went against him, and he made sure they knew he wasn't fucking around.

He wouldn't share his boy, and every motherfucker knew it; if they didn't, they learned quickly and painfully.

"No more fighting tonight," Bull's deep, gravelly voice jolted him out of his thoughts.

"I'm not—"

"I know that look, and it's never good."

Crave shot a glance at the silver haired man and found Bull's glare promising retribution. Bull had worked there even longer than him. He called the grumpy bastard one of his best friends, but Bull wasn't a man to fuck with no matter how long they'd been friends.

"I've gotten enough shit, Bull."

"Listen, we don't fight amongst ourselves. That shit is for the ring, remember it."

Oh, he remembered, he'd tangled with Bull and Psycho, even Tank and Scary a few times. At Bull's they settled arguments in the boxing ring Bull had set up in the barn. When the fight ended, they left it on the mat.

"Psycho came after me."

"I already talked to him. This shit won't keep happening. I ain't the parent here."

"I got it, no need—"

"Definitely a need since you threatened that fucker because he flirted with Twitch. Don't try to deny it because I saw you smile when he threw the punch. I ain't saying nothing about it, but either you take care of claiming your boy, or you let him go."

Again he wasn't given a chance to respond, and Bull disappeared.

His secret was out, fuck. Hopefully Bull would keep it to himself. There was only so much he could take from his co-workers and friends. He had to live with these people, even Twitch took up residence in what became known as Brawlers Farm.

His control was slim on a good day, nonexistent any other time. Crave already caught Twitch sneaking out on several nights over the past couple of months. He was positive there was someone out there he couldn't threaten. Some strange man putting his hands on Twitch—fucking Twitch. The beautiful man didn't know it yet but Crave owned him. His fists clenched so hard his knuckles cracked. He growled low in his chest and caused two men leaving to jump. He didn't apologize, something in their retreat satisfied him.

He just had to find Twitch's boyfriend, destroy the motherfucker, and prove to Twitch Crave was the man for him. Easy, right?